"So," Z_____
"who are you?"

"Isn't that a little direct?" Jane asked, a half smile on her lips as he finished pouring the champagne and held it toward her. She stared at the glass for a moment, working out how she could take it without touching his hands, but they were *big* hands and they gripped almost the entire fragile glass.

In the end, she stopped hesitating and reached out, ignoring the frisson of shock that ran through her veins when her flesh connected with his. Her eyes, though, lifted and her mouth went dry. His smile was knowing, and arrogant. The perfect antidote to her natural, genuine reactions.

He thought he'd already won her over. He was used to this—walking into the bar, being all suave and gorgeous—and getting whatever the hell he wanted from whomever he met. Well, he was about to meet his match.

A thrilling new duet from Harlequin Presents author Clare Connelly.

A Greek Inheritance Game

Who will be first down the aisle?

Zeus Papandreo was set to take over his family's billion-dollar business. But he was in for some surprises... Zeus has an illegitimate half sister, Charlotte—and she's eligible to challenge his inheritance! Worse still? Ancient bylaws dictate the sole owner of the Papandreo Group must be married. So, whoever gets to the altar first will secure the ultimate prize... The race for a ring is on!

Zeus *will* claim the company. But his search for an on-paper bride is derailed by stunning, captivating Jane... Who, unbeknownst to him, was sent by Charlotte to stall and seduce him! Yet faced with Zeus's overwhelming magnetism, *Jane*'s the one at the Greek's mercy...

Read Zeus's story
Billion-Dollar Dating Deception
Available now!

Charlotte will do anything to win—and destroy—her cruel father's legacy. And long-term lover Dante would make the perfect convenient groom. After all, they're physically compatible! But if the billionaire is to be convinced, he has terms of his own...

Read Charlotte's story
Tycoon's Terms of Engagement
Coming soon!

BILLION-DOLLAR DATING DECEPTION

CLARE CONNELLY

Harlequin
PRESENTS

If you purchased this book without a cover you should be aware that this book is stolen property. It was reported as "unsold and destroyed" to the publisher, and neither the author nor the publisher has received any payment for this "stripped book."

Harlequin® PRESENTS™

ISBN-13: 978-1-335-21323-5

Billion-Dollar Dating Deception

Copyright © 2025 by Clare Connelly

All rights reserved. No part of this book may be used or reproduced in any manner whatsoever without written permission.

Without limiting the author's and publisher's exclusive rights, any unauthorized use of this publication to train generative artificial intelligence (AI) technologies is expressly prohibited.

This is a work of fiction. Names, characters, places and incidents are either the product of the author's imagination or are used fictitiously. Any resemblance to actual persons, living or dead, businesses, companies, events or locales is entirely coincidental.

For questions and comments about the quality of this book, please contact us at CustomerService@Harlequin.com.

TM and ® are trademarks of Harlequin Enterprises ULC.

Harlequin Enterprises ULC
22 Adelaide St. West, 41st Floor
Toronto, Ontario M5H 4E3, Canada
www.Harlequin.com

Printed in Lithuania

MIX
Paper | Supporting responsible forestry
FSC® C021394

Recycling programs for this product may not exist in your area.

Clare Connelly was raised in small-town Australia among a family of avid readers. She spent much of her childhood up a tree, Harlequin book in hand. Clare is married to her own real-life hero, and they live in a bungalow near the sea with their two children. She is frequently found staring into space—a surefire sign she is in the world of her characters. She has a penchant for French food and ice-cold champagne, and Harlequin novels continue to be her favorite-ever books. Writing for Harlequin Presents is a long-held dream. Clare can be contacted via clareconnelly.com or on her Facebook page.

Books by Clare Connelly

Harlequin Presents

Twelve Nights in the Prince's Bed
Pregnant Before the Proposal
Unwanted Royal Wife
Billion-Dollar Secret Between Them

The Long-Lost Cortéz Brothers

The Secret She Must Tell the Spaniard
Desert King's Forbidden Temptation

Brooding Billionaire Brothers

The Sicilian's Deal for "I Do"
Contracted and Claimed by the Boss

The Diamond Club

His Runaway Royal

Royally Tempted

Twins for His Majesty

Visit the Author Profile page
at Harlequin.com for more titles.

To Kel, a bestie I would do anything for,
the Lottie to my Jane, and my forever SLSM.

PROLOGUE

ZEUS PAPANDREO HAD always loved the way the moonlight hit the dark timber floors of his father's study. As a young boy, he'd stood in this very same spot, looking out on the distant ocean, imagining that instead of being confined to an office, he was on a boat, at sea, free and wild, king of the ocean—king of everything.

Power had throbbed through him, even then.

Power, strength, determination.

In contrast, on this night he felt impotent. Robbed not only of his sense of power, but also of breath.

'She's twenty-three.'

Zeus closed his eyes against that, wishing his father had chosen another way to deliver this news. In writing? Over the phone? Anything that would have given him a little longer to absorb the body-blow-like information before responding.

'Her name is Charlotte.'

He wanted to punch something. To shake something, or someone. His father. He whirled around, obsidian eyes sparkling with ruthless distaste as he quickly did the requisite calculations.

'You are telling me you cheated on my mother, while she was in chemotherapy?'

Aristotle Papandreo paled perceptibly. 'It was not... Yes. I cheated.' The confession seemed to sap the older man of strength completely. He dropped his head forward, chin connecting to his chest.

A muscle jerked in Zeus's jaw. Three months ago his mother had died, after a decades-long struggle with cancer. A fight she'd taken head-on, waged countless battles against, determined to eke out as much of her life as she could, even when that life caused her so much pain in the end. Her courage and strength had been monumental, and Zeus couldn't help but draw his own strength from her.

Zeus swore loudly, the word satisfyingly crisp in the darkness of the office.

Aristotle flinched.

'And the *woman*,' he infused the word with disgust, 'that you slept with conceived a child.'

'Your sister.'

'Don't!' Zeus cursed once more. 'Don't call her that.'

'She is your sister, Zeus. She should know that.'

A muscle throbbed in Zeus's jaw as he clenched his teeth together. He strode to his father's liquor cabinet and poured a generous measure of Scotch.

'I couldn't tell you this while your mother—'

'She never knew?'

'Of course not.' Now it was Aristotle's turn to mutter something dark. 'I could never have put her through that.'

Zeus's eyes glittered. 'But sleeping with anything in a skirt was fine?'

'There was only one,' Aristotle corrected, holding up his finger.

'Oh, well, in that case, it's totally fine.'

'You do not know what it was like back then, Zeus.'

'Don't I?' He threw back a handy swig of Scotch, continuing to stare down his father. 'I was nine, but I remember.'

Aristotle glanced down at his hands. 'Mariah—Charlotte's mother... It wasn't planned.'

'I do not want to hear about it.'

'She is your sister,' Aristotle said again, more firmly. 'And it's time for her to become a part of this family.'

Zeus held the Scotch glass so firmly he was surprised it didn't shatter. 'Not my family.'

'I am meeting with my lawyers next week to go over things. I want to ensure she has what is owed to her.'

Zeus straightened.

'You're talking about leaving money to her?' Money, he didn't care about. Money, they had more than enough of.

'She is a Papandreo,' Aristotle insisted. 'This is her birthright, too.' Aristotle waved around the room, but they both knew he wasn't talking about the mansion in which they stood, but rather, the company that had been in their family for generations.

'You've got to be kidding me.' Zeus expelled a slow, angry breath. 'This is *my* birthright. Not hers. Mine.'

'She is your—'

'Don't. Just because you couldn't keep it in your pants twenty-three years ago, does not mean you can foist her on me now.'

'Oh, and you're one to talk?' Aristotle demanded sharply, for Zeus's dating history was littered with a string of short-term affairs. The older man expelled a rough sigh, dragged a hand through his hair, as if to reset himself. 'Have you forgotten the terms of company ownership, Zeus?'

Zeus squared his shoulders, meeting his father's gaze without hesitation. The antiquated term of company ownership was something he had never given much thought to, for the simple reason there'd never been anyone else in contention to inherit it. At sixty-five, his father was still young, and fit, and though Zeus had taken over the role of CEO some five years earlier, his father remained active in the company.

So the fact that some ancient Papandreo forebear, hundreds of years earlier, had had it written into the legal documentation of the company that the sole owner of Papandreo Group, as it was now known, had to be married had been neither here nor there to Zeus. For one thing, he had many years to find someone he could be bothered marrying. For another, there was no one else with a legal claim on the business who might challenge his inheritance.

At least, there hadn't been.

'That is an ancient, stupid term,' he muttered. 'No way would it stand up in court today.'

'I have tried to change it,' Aristotle said. 'It cannot be done.'

'I don't believe you.'

'Then do your best. Change it. Either way, Charlotte is my daughter, and I owe it to her to explain all of this.'

'You are saying that if she were to marry before me, you would be happy for her to inherit this? To run it, rather than me?'

'My preference would be for you to work together,' Aristotle contradicted.

'Impossible,' Zeus spat. 'She is nothing to me.' He slashed his hand angrily through the air. 'Nothing but proof of your infidelity.'

'You are angry—'

'No kidding.'

'I understand. I'm angry, too. I have been angry with myself for a long time, for that weakness of character. I did everything I could to hide Charlotte away, to spare your mother the pain of knowing what I'd done. But she's gone now, Zeus, and Charlotte deserves to come home.'

A muscle jerked low in his jaw.

'As for the company...' Aristotle looked at his son with something like sadness. 'If you are determined to be the one to inherit it, then you know what you must do.'

Zeus was very still as the reality of that splintered through him, shocking him to the core with a visceral sense of rejection.

'Marry someone?'

'Before she does,' Aristotle confirmed.

'She's twenty-three.'

'Yes, true. But who knows what she'll think when presented with the chance of stepping into a multibillion-dollar business...'

Zeus felt as though the wind had been knocked from

his sails. Wasn't it highly likely that she'd jump through whatever damned hoops were necessary to secure the company? Who wouldn't? It was like winning the lottery a million times over. He closed his eyes on a wave of disgust.

'You should have told me this sooner.'

'I couldn't. Not until—'

'My mother died,' Zeus said, crossing his arms over his chest, refusing to feel sympathy for his father. A man he had, until ten minutes ago, loved with every fibre of his being. A man Zeus would have said and done anything for, even laid down his own life. 'You disgust me,' he said, shaking his head, and with that, he stormed from the room, slamming the door behind him for good measure.

But he could not so easily box away the tangle of thoughts his father's pronouncement had given him, nor the sense of vulnerability that was tugging at his previously unassailable world view.

He was Zeus Papandreo, born to step into his father's shoes. His father, who had been almost godlike to Zeus until this night, when he learned he was mortal, after all.

He'd cheated.

Had another child with the woman he'd bedded.

You're one to talk.

After all, it wasn't as though Zeus lived like a monk. Far from it. If he'd bothered keeping the phone numbers of all the women he'd slept with, his phone would have run out of memory long ago. Which made the whole idea of marriage even less palatable. It was absurd.

Even when it was absolutely, utterly necessary. And

suddenly, it wasn't just about stepping into his birthright; it was about keeping it from his father's love child; it was about hurting his father. It was about being king of the world, king of this empire and calling the shots.

He was Zeus Papandreo and in this, he would be unstoppable.

'Lottie, you can't do it,' Jane groaned, shaking her head from side to side so her long blond hair fluffed around her pretty, heart-shaped face. 'You can't marry someone you don't know.'

'Why not?' Lottie whirled around, hands on slender hips. 'Do you have any idea what that company's worth?'

'I know it's worth a *lot*,' Jane admitted. 'But so what? You have money.'

'I have some money,' Lottie muttered. 'But not *that* kind of money.'

Jane looked at her childhood best friend with a sinking feeling, because the expression on Lottie's face was nothing short of determined. And she knew from experience that when Lottie looked like that, there was simply no talking her down. Only, something about this wasn't adding up.

'What's going on? You've *never* wanted anything from him. You live *here*, in my tiny second bedroom, borrow my clothes, freeload off my streaming services, rather than digging into that ample trust fund and buying your own place or paying for any of that stuff yourself.'

Lottie's green eyes glittered with something more familiar to Jane, a look of impishness that reminded her of the time they'd crept out of their dormitories and into the kitchen of their prestigious boarding school, to steal all the ice cream for their dorm. They'd been fourteen years old, and it had earned them the adoration of every girl in that wing for the rest of their school careers.

'Maybe it's not about the money,' Lottie said with a lift of her shoulders and a crease of her brow.

'So, what is it, then?'

Lottie pursed her wide red lips, before reaching for her coffee and taking a sip. Though she'd been raised by her English mother, and was the quintessential English rose with her pale skin, wide-set green eyes and chestnut-red hair, there was no escaping the fact that certain traits in Lottie were pure Greek. Like her predilection for strong, tar-like coffee at all hours of the day.

'All my life, they've ignored me,' she said, the words blanked of emotion, but Jane heard it, regardless. Or perhaps it was echoes of the past. Of the way she knew that rejection had shaped Lottie, had wounded her. It was something they shared. Though Jane had two parents who acknowledged her in their lives, they had barely any time to give her, other than a few perfunctory holidays each year. They had paid for a nanny to watch her graduate high school and send them photographs. Though outwardly, both Charlotte and Jane had always projected an image of untouchable contentment to the world, to one another, they were honest. Each knew the truth. Rejection was awful, and they'd both suffered through more than enough of it.

'I know,' Jane murmured, sympathetically.

'And now he's telling me I can have the family business, if I want it. That I'm just as entitled to it as Zeus.'

She layered the word with contempt, and Jane could well understand it. Where Lottie had been forced to live her life in hiding, never telling anyone who her father was—courtesy of the nondisclosure agreement Aristotle Papandreo had forced Lottie's mother to sign, in exchange for a huge payoff—Zeus had been in the spotlight as the much-adored sole son and heir to the Papandreo fortune.

'I never wanted it,' she said with a twist of her lips and a flash of those sea-green eyes. 'I would have said I hated the thought of it, until I realised I could reach out and take it, after all.'

'But why do you want it?' Jane pushed.

'Think of what we could do with that thing,' Lottie murmured, crossing the room and crouching in front of her oldest, closest friend. Lottie's hands closed over Jane's, who sighed softly. 'Think of the *good* we could do with it.'

Jane gnawed on her lower lip, as thousands of late-night conversations flooded her brain. All the ideas they'd had over the years, for ways to help the less advantaged. Neither had ever really felt as though they belonged in the elite school community they'd attended. They were different to the other girls, and their strong sense of social conscience had driven both to pursue careers in the charity and not-for-profit sector, upon leaving school.

'With you and me at the helm of the Papandreo Group, we could turn it on its head. Instead of seeking a gross amount of profits, we could make it our mission to divest. *Everything.*'

Jane gasped. 'You're talking about destroying it.'

'Yes.' Lottie's face tightened with renewed determination. 'It's obscene for anyone to have that kind of money.'

Jane didn't disagree.

'But not just to be spiteful,' Lottie promised. 'Don't get me wrong. I would enjoy every damned minute of pulling apart that business and selling it off and seeing the expressions on their faces as I did so,' she said, cheeks flushed now at the very idea. 'Mostly, though, it's about the good we could do. This is everything we've always said we wanted, Jane. Everything.'

And it was. A thousand of their plans suddenly seemed viable and within reach. Jane's breath came a little faster.

'Okay.' She squeezed Lottie's hand. Because, when it came down to it, there was nothing she wouldn't do for her very best friend in the whole world. They'd been through too much together, knew too much about one another's lives, pains, weaknesses, to ever walk away in a moment of need. 'How can I help?'

'I'm glad you asked, because actually, I *do* need your help…'

CHAPTER ONE

JANE'S LEGS WERE wobbling a week later, as she strode into the sleekly glamorous bar in the expensive business district of central Athens. Not from nerves, but from the experience of wearing sky-high heels for the first time in years. In fact, the whole outfit was well and truly outside of Jane's comfort zone. She'd borrowed the whole ensemble from Lottie—who was far more at home in the latest fashions and had an eye for snatching things up from thrift shops, to meet her self-imposed budgetary restraints. At first, she'd thought she would be overdressed in the silky gold camisole top tucked into a white miniskirt, with strappy leather stilettos and a chunky golden necklace, but two steps into the bar and she saw that Lottie had chosen the perfect outfit.

This was not like their local Clapham pub, that was for sure. This place screamed highbrow, from the leather banquettes to the classy art on the walls and the subdued lighting.

She fought an urge to bite onto her lip, the gesture one of uncertainty that didn't belong with this persona. Tonight she was Jane Fisher, confident daughter of one of the world's most renowned human rights lawyers, graduate of an elite British public school and university, ready to take on the world.

Or rather, Zeus Papandreo.

'I just need you to flirt with him a bit,' Lottie had explained. 'Make him, you know, fall in love with you.'

Jane had immediately balked. 'I can't just make him fall in love with me!'

Lottie snorted then. 'Tell me the last time you looked at a guy twice who didn't immediately want you to have his babies?'

Jane's cheeks had flushed at her friend's description. For Jane, who hated attention, she'd cursed the fact, many times over, that she'd inherited her socialite mother's looks. Especially after Steven. 'You know I don't do serious.'

'I know that, but he doesn't. And he'll be just as fallible to your charms as everyone else, I promise.'

'How long do I need to do this for?'

'Until I'm married,' Lottie promised. 'And believe me, I plan to work fast.'

Jane's jaw had dropped. 'You're serious?'

'Don't worry. I'll find someone suitable.'

'Suitable? In weeks?'

'How hard can it be? You get proposed to all the time,' Lottie teased, then winced, because Jane had been proposed to twice, and both times had been disastrous—for Jane, who hated hurting anybody. 'Sorry.'

She shook her head. 'So, I just have to...'

'Well, the way I see it, he's going to be looking to get married, too,' Lottie explained. 'So, you just need to

make him think you're swallowing his act. He'll probably be super charming, move quickly, so it won't be hard. Just get him to think you're buying it, that you're keen to get married, but keep coming up with reasons to put it off—wanting your parents to meet him, that kind of thing. Basically, stall. Stall, stall, stall.'

And Jane had nodded, because how hard would that be? She just had to stop him from trying to hook up with anyone else and get them to marry him. Surely, she could do that?

'You'll have him eating out of the palm of your hand within hours—right where I need him. And I'll owe you forever. I am sorry to ask this of you, Jane. I know... I know it will be hard for you. But you're the only person I can trust. The only person who loves me enough to help me.'

Surreptitiously, Jane scanned the bar, looking for a glimpse of the man she now knew like the back of her hand, courtesy of Lottie and her wine-fuelled internet searching. They knew this bar was around the corner from his office, and that he'd been photographed leaving here with many beautiful women over the past few years, since he'd taken over as CEO of the Papandreo Group.

Unseating him from that role was the first thing on Lottie's list, and Jane couldn't say she blamed her friend. For the more she'd read about Zeus Papandreo, the less she liked him. While she was motivated primarily by helping her friend, she also couldn't resist the idea of taking him down a peg or two, for the sake of womankind. Men like him, who went through women as though they were worthless and good for one thing only, definitely deserved to have the tables turned from time to time. Out of nowhere, she thought of Steven—damn it, the last man she wanted to think of here and now—and her heart gave a familiar twist of pain, as sharp as it had been back then, as a seventeen-year-old, when he'd shattered it—and her—into a million pieces.

There was that old adage about time healing all wounds, but that was certainly not the case for Jane.

That particular emotional bruise was as tender now as it had been six years earlier. So, too, the pain her parents had inflicted over the years.

In her experience, some hurts just couldn't be eased. It was better to accept that than try to fight it.

A low whistle caught her attention, and she glanced towards the bar, where two suited men were looking at her as though they'd just fronted up to a buffet and she was the main attraction. 'Can we buy you a drink?'

'No, thank you.' She glanced beyond them. No sign of Zeus, so far. She strode beyond the men, not looking at them again, and found an empty spot down the other end. She ordered a mineral water—all the better to keep her wits about her. She opened up one of the news apps on her phone and began to read a long article on an overseas war, her gut rolling as the atrocities were described, and she felt that same yearning she'd known all her life to help.

'You're just like your father,' her mother had cooed once, and Jane had shied away from the comparison, even when it had, on some level, pleased her. Because her father had definitely wanted to help the world. He had taken cases all over, fighting for the underprivileged, doing everything he could to make their lives better. But his calling for justice was so strong that he'd forgotten all about the daughter he was leaving to be raised in utter luxury—by nannies, household staff and boarding-school mothers.

It wasn't much later when something made the hairs on the back of Jane's neck stand on end. Though the crowd in the bar didn't actually stop talking, she felt an eerie sense of silence descend, or her ears grew woolly, and she glanced up towards the door and saw the moment Zeus Papandreo strode in, every bit as world-owning as she had expected. Only, in that moment of crossing the threshold, before entering the bar, she saw something else, too. Something she was perhaps projecting onto him.

A look of burden.

A sense that he was carrying more than his fair share of worries.

A sense of brokenness.

It was gone in an instant, so thoroughly replaced by a look of arrogant command, that she thought she must have imagined it. He strode to the bar, easily clearing the way despite how crowded it was, gesturing towards the top of the shelves at a bottle of Scotch.

The barman, dressed in a white button-up shirt and vest turned, retrieved the bottle and poured a measure, sliding it across to Zeus with a polite nod.

Zeus took it, rested one elbow on the bar top and began to survey the room, just as Jane had done when she'd entered. She watched as he took notice of a group of women in the corner dressed in corporate clothes, so she presumed they'd come straight from the office. She saw the way his eyes lingered there a moment, one corner of his mouth lifting appreciatively, and her heart skipped a beat.

Showtime.

She straightened a little, pulling her silky blond hair over one shoulder, and positioning herself so the generous curve of her breasts against the silk of her camisole would be easily noticeable. Sure enough, the two men who'd offered to buy her a drink earlier glanced her way and she felt heat infuse her cheeks. For all she was willing to play the part of the vixen for Lottie, it was not a role Jane was particularly comfortable with.

She ran a finger down the side of her mineral water, making a show of tracing the condensation, then lifting her moist finger towards her mouth at the exact moment Zeus's glance shifted over her. And back again. Their eyes met, but she didn't slow her finger's progress, even when the charge of realisation was akin to an electric shock.

His eyes.

His eyes were so...intense.

Dark and brooding, and beautifully shaped, with the kind of lashes she thought only existed in romance novels and movies, thick and dark and curling, giving the impression that he wore eyeliner.

They bore into her as though with just one look he could see the finer points of her soul.

She pressed her fingertip to her lips, let it hover there

a moment before dropping it to the bar and offering a slightly dismissive smile. Coming on too strong with a man like Zeus wouldn't work, she guessed. He was someone who liked to be in charge, who liked to do the chasing, and she somehow just knew that he would have been prey to enough money-hungry gold diggers in his time to spot one a mile off.

Play it cool, Lottie had advised, echoing Jane's own judgement. *Let him think he has to work for you. It will kill him. And he's so damned stubborn, he won't give up until he thinks he's got you right where he wants you.*

Jane sipped her mineral water, manicured nails curved around the cut-crystal glass, as the nearest bartender uncorked a bottle of expensive champagne and placed it in a cooler with two glasses. Jane returned her attention to her phone, but it didn't last long. A moment later, the champagne ice bucket was placed directly in front of her. 'Compliments of the gentleman over there,' the barman said, nodding towards Zeus.

Her pulse flickered to life as she made a point of slowly, oh, so slowly, scanning the guests assembled at the bar before letting her gaze land on his face. One of his brows quirked upwards in a silent, flirtatious question. She responded in kind, offering a wry half smile and a 'please explain' expression.

No need to ask twice.

He strolled through the busy bar easily, but the bar itself was busy enough that in order to be next to her, he had to slide in close. So close she could feel his warmth and smell his tangy aftershave. So close she could see those magnificent eyes up close and marvel at the obsidian darkness of them. For a moment, she felt a rush of guilt for the deception she was about to try to perpetrate. But only a moment. Because wasn't he doing exactly the same thing?

Lottie had explained the arcane inheritance clause very carefully. It wasn't just Lottie who needed to get married in order to legally inherit the Papandreo Group, but Zeus as well. Meaning he was out here, no doubt looking for some poor woman he could con into agreeing to marry him, never mind how that might end up breaking her heart. If anything, Jane was doing her sisters a solid by foiling those plans. Because it would be much more devastating for a woman to be used by Zeus Papandreo than it could ever be for a man to be disappointed by Jane.

'I haven't seen you here before,' he said, voice lightly accented, deep and husky. The hairs on her arms stood on end and she bit back a shiver, as he reached across her and took the champagne from the cooler, along with one of the glasses. 'May I?'

Her pulse was strangely throbbing—courtesy of the plan, she assured herself. It didn't matter *why* she felt all lightheaded, though. She could make him believe the reason was his proximity, his masculine strength, his obvious attractiveness.

'Thank you,' she agreed, nodding once.

'So,' he asked, pouring the glass, 'who are you?'

'Isn't that a little direct?' she asked, a half smile on her lips as he finished pouring the champagne and held it towards her. She stared at the glass for a moment, working out how she could take it without touching his hands, but they were *big* hands, and they gripped almost the entire fragile glass.

In the end, she stopped hesitating and reached out, ignoring the frisson of shock that ran through her veins when her flesh connected with his. Her eyes, though, lifted, and her mouth went dry. His smile was knowing and arrogant. The perfect antidote to her natural, genuine reactions.

He thought he'd already won her over. He was used to this—walking into the bar, being all suave and gorgeous and getting whatever the hell he wanted from whomever he met. Well, he was about to meet his match.

'I happen to like direct,' he said, lifting one shoulder. 'Don't you—?' He let the sentence hang, midconstruction, in the air between them, and when she didn't fill the gap, he asked, 'What is your name?'

She pulled her lips to the side, thinking how commanding he was, how he seemed to think he could walk up to anyone and begin interrogating them.

'You tell me yours and I'll tell you mine,' she said, enjoying the way his features briefly reflected surprise.

'You don't know who I am?'

'Should I?' She batted her lashes then sipped the champagne, enjoying the rush of ice-cold bubbles as they filled her mouth and then flooded her body.

He frowned. 'I suppose not.'

'Are you famous?' she pushed, enjoying teasing him.

'No.'

'Then why would I know who you are? Or have we perhaps met?'

His laugh then was a gruff sound of genuine amusement. 'I think we'd both remember.'

'You're certainly not lacking in confidence, are you—?' She used his intonation, inflecting a slight question at the end of her words.

'Zeus,' he responded, almost brushing aside his name. 'And I think you'll find I'm not lacking in lots of things.'

Her own laugh was—to her chagrin and surprise—also genuine. 'Does this usually work for you?' she purred, taking another sip of champagne before placing the glass down and putting her elbow on the bar, propping her chin in her palm so she could lean a little closer to him.

He scanned her face. 'Are you saying you're not interested?'

Careful, Jane.

She wanted to push him, without pushing him away. 'Hmm,' she murmured, reaching for her hair and stroking it. 'I'm not saying that, exactly,' she said, after a pulse had throbbed between them. 'I did ask your name, after all.'

'That's true and promised your own in exchange.'

'Jane,' she said, wondering why it seemed as though the simple act of uttering her name was somehow akin to the throwing down of a gauntlet. Blood seemed to pound far too fast through her veins, so she was intimately familiar with the fragility of her body's construction, the paper-thin vascular walls that suddenly might not be able to contain the torrent of her body's pulse.

'Jane,' he repeated, and the same pulse she'd been worried about seconds earlier seemed to rush even

faster. He said it like a promise; he said it like a curse.
'It doesn't suit you,' he said, tilting his head a little.

Her stomach dropped to her toes. Only Charlotte knew that Jane had, in fact, been christened Boudica Jane—a glimpse into her parents' aspirations for her. To save the world, by following in their footsteps. If only they'd held her hand and allowed her to walk a little more closely.

'Disappointed?' she deflected, in no way interested in revealing her true name to this man. She had dropped the Boudica in the third grade, when a girl in her class had taken to calling her 'booger digger'—naturally, it had caught on and she'd lived with the moniker for years.

'No. I'm sure I can think of something else to call you.'

His tone was undeniably intimate, husky with promise. She glanced away, cheeks flushing at the imagery his nearness and voice were provoking, so her eyes landed on one of the two men down the bar who'd offered to buy her a drink earlier. Zeus hadn't offered, she realised, so much as bought the drink and walked over as though that were his God-given right. The difference between him and mere mortals, she thought with a hint of a sneer.

The man down the bar winked at her.

'Friends of yours?'

She turned back to Zeus. 'No.'

'Though they wish they were?'

She lifted a shoulder. 'I can't say.'

'Why do I get the feeling I'm dealing with someone who's left a trail of broken hearts behind her?'

'Why do I get the feeling I'm dealing with someone who doesn't believe in a heart's function?'

He laughed again and she ignored the whisper of delight that breathed through her at that, at how much she liked hearing his spontaneous humour.

'*Touché*,' he said, reaching not for the empty champagne flute and topping it up, but rather lifting hers and taking a sip from it, whilst holding her gaze. Her pulse went into dangerous territory now. 'What if you're wrong?'

'I don't think I am.'

'I thought you didn't know who I am?'

'I've known men like you before.'

'I doubt that.'

'Arrogant, handsome, successful,' she enumerated, but with a slow smile to show that she was teasing. Flirting. Baiting... 'Tell me I'm wrong.'

'Why tell you, when showing you would be so much more fun?'

Her heart galloped along. 'How do you suggest doing that?'

'Well,' he said, leaning closer, holding her champagne flute. 'Let's start with a drink and go from there.'

The promise in the latter part of that sentence was exactly what she both dreaded and needed. A promise for more, because that was how she was going to hook Lottie's nemesis and keep him distracted, but also, now that she was face-to-face with Zeus Papandreo, she freely admitted that it was going to be harder to control this thing than she'd initially anticipated.

Jane had considered her heart—and libido—to have

been iced over six years earlier, with that awful heartbreak in her final year of school, but in fact, she was learning, on this night of all nights, that there was at least one man who was capable of reviving the latter. For there was no denying the heat flooding her body was pooling between her legs, and that if he were to glance down, she suspected he'd notice the way her nipples had grown taut beneath the flimsy material of her bra.

'A drink,' she heard herself purr, glad that love and loyalty to Lottie had reasserted itself. 'And after that, we'll see...'

CHAPTER TWO

AT FIRST GLANCE, THE BAR had appeared to be a rectangular room with timber walls and windows on one side that looked out onto a busy, restaurant precinct street. But with Jane's acceptance of sharing a drink with him, Zeus had nodded swiftly, put a hand in the small of her back and guided her away from the bar and through the crowd, towards a wide set of doors she hadn't initially noticed.

'It's more private in here,' he said, leaning down closer to her ear when he spoke, because it was loud, and the warmth of his breath made her whole-body tingle. She forced herself to focus, to regain control of her wayward senses.

'All the better to hear me with?'

'Hear you, see you...'

'Blow my house down?' she couldn't resist volleying back.

'As you said, we'll see,' he promised, and the words were so unmistakably sensual that her whole body seemed to catch fire. The hand in the small of her back was warm and he moved it a little upwards. She glanced at him then, at the exact moment his eyes dropped to her lips, and she felt as though the world had stopped spinning.

They stood perfectly still, in the middle of the private area of the bar. Jane was dimly aware of a few other tables of guests, but she couldn't properly register them, nor hear anything other than a general din of noise. In the centre of her mind, and in every peripheral space as well, there was only Zeus.

'I—' She sought to fill the silence, to blot out the awareness that was humming through her, because this was supposed to be a ruse, and she was meant to be playing the part of someone like her mother. Beautiful, sophisticated, wealthy and with a casual attitude to sex and relationships. Instead, she found herself slipping back into her real self, into Jane Fisher, virtually orphaned, unloved, bullied as a child, broken-hearted at seventeen and afterwards, terrified of and turned off by sex. Those wounds had cut deep, and now, opposite Zeus, she felt a bundle of insecurities.

'Come and sit with me, Jane,' he said, but there was almost a hint of resignation in his tone. Of something that didn't, in fact, make sense. Until she remembered that if she were faux husband hunting, then he was doing the same: looking for a woman he could con into marriage.

Resignation, because he didn't want to marry.

Resignation, because he needed to flirt with someone until they couldn't say no to his charms and would agree to anything he proposed.

Resignation, because this was all fake—for him, absolutely—and he almost couldn't be bothered with it.

But for the trillion-dollar empire he viewed solely as his birthright, what wouldn't he do?

Love for Lottie had Jane straightening her spine, and finally, she was in control again, able to tamp down on the fast-moving current of sexual attraction and focus on the end goal. Distract, distract, distract. Thwart, thwart, thwart.

This wasn't a big deal. Men like Zeus were so used to thinking they could take whatever they wanted, regardless of who got hurt. Well, it was past time for him to learn his lesson, and Jane would relish giving it to him.

'Where?' She made a show of blinking up at him, her own long lashes flicking against the softness of her cheeks.

He gestured towards a booth in the corner, dimly lit and private.

Her heart trembled despite her assertion moments ago that she was back in charge. But she didn't convey a hint of her doubt. Instead, she turned on her stiletto heel and walked steadily towards the booth, sliding all the way along, into the corner.

It was only when she sat down that she realised he hadn't brought their drinks with them, and her throat was parched and her nerves in desperate need of stilling.

No matter—almost seconds later, with a flick of his fingers, a bartender appeared.

'What will you have?'

'I—was fine with the champagne in there,' Jane pointed out.

'Champagne,' he said, then turned to face her, placing his elbow on the table and his other arm along the back of the banquette seat, so he effectively caged her in the breadth of his body. After Steven, Jane had been terrified of dominant men. She'd tried dating a few times, but had gravitated towards slim, slight cerebral types. Men who couldn't hurt her. Men she could defend herself against. Zeus certainly didn't fit that mould, and yet she wasn't afraid. At least, she wasn't afraid of him. The fear that was trembling at the base of her spine had more to do with the force of want pulsating inside her.

She stared across at him, half wanting to back out of this—even when she knew she never could.

'You're buying another bottle?'

'You want more?'

'There's a bottle open on the bar in there.'

'Would you like me to go and get it?'

'It just seems a little wasteful.'

'I'm not bothered.'

She didn't act quickly enough to suppress her sneer. Yes, she'd known men like him before. So carelessly wealthy, so utterly taking their ridiculous bank balances for granted. They never realised what a difference that money could make to the less fortunate.

The waiter returned with a champagne bottle and two glasses. When he went to open it in front of them, Zeus took the bottle and waved the server away in that manner of his that was pure 'I am king, hear me command.'

'Well, Zeus,' she drawled as he uncorked the champagne and poured two glasses. 'Tell me about yourself.'

He quirked a teasing expression in her direction, then lifted his glass in a silent salute. She reached for her own, clinking them together.

'To new friends,' he murmured.

'And old ones,' she added, thinking of Lottie like a touchstone now, aware that she had to focus on her loyalty to the other woman so as not to quit this harebrained scheme.

He dipped his head once, apparently accepting her amendment, then took a sip. 'What would you like to know?'

'Do you work near here?'

'Yes.'

Her lips flickered into a smile, then tightened when he glanced down, his eyes staring at her mouth in a way that made them tingle. The room was not warm, and yet Jane's body was. She felt awash with heat and sipped the ice-cold champagne gratefully.

'Where?'

'Two blocks away.'

Jane rolled her eyes at his vagueness. 'What do you do?'

'I'm in a family business.'

'How quaint,' she responded, intentionally goading him. 'Do you work with your parents?'

'My father retired five years ago,' he said. 'And my mother died in the spring.'

Jane's grip on her champagne flute almost faltered. She'd known that, though she'd temporarily forgotten. The way he said it pulled hard on her heart.

'I'm sorry.' The response was dragged from deep within her. She reached out and put a hand on his knee, surprising herself with the need to offer comfort. 'That must have been very hard.'

He nodded once, sipped his champagne, looking away, and Jane could have cursed. She wished she hadn't seen this side of him, this glimpse of humanity, because it would have been easier to ensure she didn't feel anything for Zeus as humanising as pity.

He was someone she had to bait into a fake relationship, and in order to achieve that, she had to continue to regard him as her best friend's nemesis and nothing more. That was easy when he was flirting like it was a professional sport, and looking at her in the same way those other men in the bar had. But when he said something so intimate, how could she not soften, just a little? Just for a moment?

'What brings you to Athens?'

The change of subject was swift and slightly disconcerting, because she was still wrapped up in sympathy and softness for him, whereas Zeus had regrouped alarmingly fast. She tried to keep up, but took a sip of champagne just to help settle those frustratingly discordant nerves.

'How do you know I don't live here?' she asked, stalling for time.

'You've never heard of me,' he pointed out.

'Okay, buster. Spill. You're obviously famous or something,' she said, glad to turn the tables and redirect conversation back to him.

'Not famous,' he disputed. 'But locally known.'

'Because you have the kind of eyes a woman could lose herself in?' She couldn't resist teasing, enjoying the way those dark eyes flashed to hers with speculation and heat.

His laugh was unsettling, though, because it shook her to her core right when she had thought she was back in control.

'Because my family has been based here for hundreds of years, run businesses out of Athens that are known all over the world.'

'You're Zeus Papandreo,' she said, glad she could at least get that out in the open, as it made her feel like less of a liar.

'Guilty as charged.'

'But you're not guilty,' she murmured. 'You're proud.'

'Yes.'

Anger fired inside her. Proud because he was a Papandreo. Proud because he belonged to that family. With no notion of the dark side of the moon, of what it had been like for Lottie to grow up shunned and hidden, with the ignominy of her conception and birth hanging over her head as though she were some dirty secret.

'I can understand why,' Jane muttered, wishing she were a slightly better liar, because she couldn't quite flatten the contempt from her tone, and Zeus was so perceptive, she was almost certain he caught it. She expelled a breath and forced a smile, trying again. 'Your family's success is remarkable.'

He shrugged. 'It's easy to be successful when you have a legacy like this behind you.'

More anger whipped inside her. Not only had this man grown up with everything at his fingertips that should have been Lottie's, he was also clearly moving the pieces in his life to marry, swiftly, to further deny Lottie what should now be hers.

Hell, if Jane hadn't already been committed to this, then she was doubly so now. She would move heaven and earth to secure Lottie's birthright, even just so Lottie could sit at the top of the tower and look down on Zeus and their father for a time. She'd earned that right, damn it.

'Modesty, Mr Papandreo?' she asked, pleased that she was able to continue acting flirtatious when she was feeling anything *but*. Except, that wasn't strictly true. Regardless of how much she hated and despised this man, because of what he'd had that Lottie should also have had, her body seemed to have its own ideas.

'Honesty. I'm secure enough in my achievements without needing to exaggerate them.'

She arched a brow, and out of nowhere, she imagined that if he was anyone else, she might actually have been halfway enjoying herself. He was such a consummate flirt; he made this easy.

'So, Jane, you're on holiday in Athens?' he prompted after a beat's silence.

'Yes,' she said, trying to remember the fib she and Lottie had concocted. They figured they needed three months to give Lottie enough time to find someone to marry and put everything in motion. Three months lined up with summer and, as luck would have it, the maternity contract Jane had been covering had finished two weeks earlier, so she was at a loose end for the next little while, anyway.

'For any reason in particular?'

'I've never been.' That, at least, was true.

'How is that possible?'

'Well, I hate to break it to you, but it's not actually the centre of the world.'

He pulled a fake wounded expression. 'But surely it's one of the most beautiful places.'

'I'll have to take your word for it,' she murmured. 'I only arrived this afternoon.'

His brows shot up. 'And you're wasting time in a bar, rather than exploring?'

'I was thirsty.'

He laughed. 'And hungry?'

'That depends. Are you asking me for dinner?'

His eyes bore into hers. 'Unfortunately, I have plans tonight.' Her heart dropped to her toes in an unexpectedly real response. Plans? She panicked. A date? With someone else? Another contender for his bride? Desperation made her lean a little closer, and she realised she still had her hand on his knee from earlier.

Go big, or go home, she thought, gliding it just an inch or so higher, as her eyes hooked to his and held.

His pants were soft to touch, but his leg muscle was tight and strong, so she couldn't help but imagine him without these pants. Imagine the way he'd be all tanned and hair roughened and… The image was making her insides swirl uncomfortably.

What are you doing? her inner Jane cried.

The inner Jane who'd kept her safe for six years by urging her to avoid men, and particularly men like Zeus. Not only was she flirting with him, baiting with him, she was also walking right into a fire, seemingly uncaring about getting burned.

'That's a shame,' she murmured as her glance fell on his lips. Her whole body tingled.

'Is it?'

'Well, for me,' she murmured, unconsciously moving closer. 'I would have liked to share dinner with a local. I'm sure you could tell me the best sights in town.'

'Like a tour guide?'

'Something like that.'

'Jane,' he said, moving then so their legs brushed beneath the table, and his much larger frame suddenly seemed not only to trap her but also to envelop her completely. In that instant, she was overwhelmed by her senses—his smell, his warmth, his closeness, the feeling of his trousers beneath her palm. But not fear. Again, she marvelled at that, because fear had seemed to be such an ingrained response in her, with so many men since Steven. Why not Zeus? 'I'd like to see you again.'

Her gut twisted. 'I thought we just agreed you'd be my tour guide.'

He nodded slowly. 'But we both know that's not what I'm talking about.'

Her heart stammered hard into her ribs. 'Isn't it?'

He arched a brow. 'Unless I'm mistaken…' And then, he mirrored her gesture, putting his hand on her bare leg just above the knee and moving a little higher. The contact was both completely welcome and utterly shocking—shocking because of how her senses screamed in immediate recognition and want. Need.

She blanked thoughts of Lottie then, trying not to imagine what her best friend would say if she knew how much Jane was enjoying this lothario's attentions.

Jane! Who'd thought no man on earth could stir anything like interest in her any longer. She hadn't felt a rush of physical attraction for *anyone* since that awful night when she'd lost control—had it taken away from her—and been truly terrified. It was as though her whole body had been put into stasis, yet now it was waking up, and waking up fast.

He moved his hand higher, slowly, eyes watching her the whole time, silently inviting her to stop him, to ask him to stop, but she didn't. Just knowing that he was watching for that relaxed her enough to enjoy this. She felt *safe*. Her lips parted and she moved a little closer, dropping her head near the curve of his neck.

His fingers crept towards her inner thigh, to the expanse of flesh revealed by the very short skirt she wore, and higher still. 'Tell me to stop,' he said, inviting her to pause this madness, his voice low and throaty.

'We're in a bar,' was all she said, but it was hardly an answer, or a problem, because they were hidden away in a corner of the bar, and his frame was large enough to hide her entirely from view.

'So we are,' he agreed, before dropping his head and finding her lips, kissing her as though it was what he'd been born to do, kissing her so that her breath burned in her lungs and her whole body exploded in an electric, binding flash of light. Kissing her at the same moment his fingers brushed the silk of her underpants and found her most sensitive cluster of nerves, teasing her there through the fabric; teasing her until she was moaning into their kiss, and her body was awash with a strange, overwhelmingly heady rush of adrenaline.

The fact they were in a bar no longer mattered—Jane couldn't have said *where* she was in space, time or life. She knew only that if he stopped touching her, she might scream. Fortunately, he didn't stop touching her, nor kissing her. She writhed her hips, eager for more, wanting him to really touch her, no longer conscious of who she was, who he was, nor what she was supposed to be doing. He moved his kiss lower, to her neck, and then held her tight against him as his fingers began to brush faster. The waves that had been building inside her hit a peak and crescendoed, and then, because she'd lost all sense of time and place, she moaned loudly, so he kissed her again to swallow the sound, kissed her as she moaned into his mouth, as sanity and pleasure seemed to burst apart, forming a thousand droplets inside her. Making her whimper, making her weak, when she'd sworn she'd never be weak again.

She pulled away from him quickly, staring at him with a look of absolute shock.

He couldn't blame her.

When was the last time he'd done anything like that? Years. Years and years. Maybe as a younger man, he might have given in to the temptations of his body and found a woman who was as driven by a need for pleasure as he was, enough to throw caution—and geography—to the wind, but Zeus was thirty-three now, and in far greater control of himself.

Or so he'd thought.

But one look at Jane…hell, he didn't even know her last name. No matter. One look at her across the room and something had slipped into place inside him; and it didn't take a genius to work out why.

The marriage ultimatum.

Zeus was not a man who enjoyed ultimatums, nor did he relish the prospect of marriage, particularly not with the woman—or the sort of woman—he had in mind. So Jane, whoever she was, was simply an act of rebellion, of acting out while he was still free to do so. A last hurrah, so to speak, before he turned his mind to what he absolutely had to do.

'Give me your number,' he demanded, pulling his phone from his pocket and putting it on the tabletop. Her cheeks were flushed, and her fingers shook. She glanced around uncertainly. Shy. Like a sweet little innocent, when he suspected the opposite was true.

But she nodded then and quickly tapped something into his phone. He took it and for good measure, pressed the call button. He heard hers begin to trill and hung up, satisfied that he would see her again.

'I—that—I don't—'

He pressed a finger to her lips, the same finger that had just been so achingly close to her sex. 'Don't explain. I felt it, too.'

Her eyes widened and her tongue darted out to lick her lips but instead connected with his finger. His gut felt as though it were filled with stones. Suddenly, the date he'd organised in response to his father's revelation was the very last thing he wanted to do.

'It's just not—'

'No explanations,' he insisted. 'I'll call you.' And because he suspected that if he were to remain for even five more seconds, he would lose the willpower to walk away altogether, he stood and left in one swift motion, refusing to look back even when he desperately wanted to.

He had more important things to consider than indulging his suddenly voracious libido. Like getting married just as soon as he could possibly arrange it.

CHAPTER THREE

Right up until an hour ago, Zeus had decided that Philomena was the perfect contender to be his bride. She was smart, incredibly ambitious, and they'd known one another for more than ten years, so he knew he could trust her. She had dated a couple of men, for around a year each, but as far as he knew, had never been seriously involved with anyone, which made him wonder if she was as averse to commitment as he was.

Most importantly, she was available and, going by her dress, interested enough to want to impress him. Which made it impossibly frustrating that he couldn't get Jane out of his mind.

Even here, sitting across from Philomena, listening to her talk about her work at a law firm a few blocks away, he could barely focus on what she was saying—and a lack of focus was *not* something Zeus generally experienced any issues with. On the contrary, he had a laser-like intensity when he turned his mind to something. And what he'd decided to turn his mind to was the imperative to marry, and fast.

Jane was a tourist. Someone he didn't know the last thing about—including her surname. So what if one look at her made his whole body aflame with desire? He'd had great sex before. Surely, he wasn't going to be led around by a certain part of his anatomy that should have known better. Not now, when the stakes were so high.

He couldn't afford to get distracted. He couldn't afford to be seen around town with Jane, if he wanted someone like Philomena to take him seriously. Which meant he should do the smart thing and delete her number off his phone. As in, an hour ago. He should have deleted it as soon as he walked out of the bar, not stared at it the entire car ride over here, as if willing *her* to call *him*.

And what if she had? Would he have ditched Philomena and the carefully laid plans for his future, all to spend one night with Jane?

He was at a juncture in his life, a turning point. Everything he had grown up to believe was his by rights was now in jeopardy. The business wasn't just a business to him, but rather, a home.

When he was nine years old and his mother received her first cancer diagnosis, he'd gone to the office with his grandfather, sat opposite him while he worked. When he was thirteen and the cancer came back, it was his father he shadowed in the holidays, learning, focusing on the business, understanding every aspect of it because it was better than thinking about his pale, slim mother and the light that was fading from her. When he was eighteen, and his mother had been in a brief period of remission, it was Zeus who took over the company for six months, while his parents went on holiday together. At twenty-one, when a new diagnosis had come, he did the same thing, allowing his father to support her through the frequent hospitalisations. The business was his sanctuary; it was *his*. Watching his mother's illness return time and time again had left him with an unshakable sense that human relationships were frail and untrustworthy, that the greatest love of all could be taken away at any point.

And yet, in the midst of that, he had known he would always have the company. He would always be the sole Papandreo heir. Ensuring that remained the case was what he should have been focused on, and only that. Not Jane.

He closed his eyes for a moment, and he saw her as she'd been at the bar. He'd been drawn to her almost the moment he'd stepped across the threshold. And who could blame him? She had the kind of beauty men went to war for, with that tumbling, lustrous blond hair and wide, curved mouth, full lips that had been painted a seductive red, wide, pretty blue eyes, high cheekbones and deep dimples when she smiled. As for her figure—

'Zeus?' Philomena reached over and put a hand on his. 'Are you well?'

He stared down at Philomena's hand and forced himself to concentrate. Too much was riding on him getting married quickly to be distracted now.

'I'm fine,' he responded, a little sharply. 'Go on.'

She frowned, but did continue speaking, much to his relief. Now, if only he could control the direction of his thoughts, because without his consent they were obsessing over Jane, so that, as the night wore on, he found his nerves were stretched well beyond breaking point.

* * *

Jane had just stepped out of the shower and was pulling on one of the fluffy hotel robes when her phone began to buzz and her pulse immediately leapt into her throat as she imagined that it might be Zeus. It was almost midnight, though. Surely, he wouldn't call this late? Only…after what had happened in the bar, could she blame him if he thought she might be up for a literal one-night stand?

Heat flushed her cheeks when she recalled the way she'd responded to his touch. No, the way she'd practically *begged* him to touch her.

And it hadn't even been about Lottie, but rather Jane's needs.

How had that happened? That night with Steven had terrified her. Up until then, they'd messed around, and she'd fallen in love with him—or thought she had. She trusted him, and she thought he'd been happy to wait, just like she'd asked. Instead, he'd plied her with alcohol and slept with her—her first and only time with a man—when she was too out of it to know what she was doing. She only remembered some of it, because of the fog of alcohol. But she knew that it had hurt, and that it had been fast and that he'd laughed off her upset afterwards. It had been a betrayal from which she could never return. Afterwards, any man's touch had left her cold at first. It had taken years before she was willing to date anyone, and she'd kissed some men, perfunctorily, and hadn't hated it, but she'd always been terrified of anything more intimate because…what if? What if they promised her something and then broke that promise?

She reached for her phone, snatching it out of her bag, face pale now, and flicked it over to see the screen. Lottie's smiling face looked back at her, the photo taken about a year earlier when they were on holiday together in Scotland. Lottie was wearing one of the telltale scarves from the Harry Potter movies—a firm favourite of both of theirs for as long as Jane could remember. She expelled a calming breath, glad to see it was Lottie and no one else.

'Hi,' she answered.

'Oh! You're there. I was about to hang up.'

'I was in the shower. Is everything okay?'

'Yeah, why?'

'It's just…late,' Jane finished with a shrug.

'Oh, shoot. I forgot the time difference. Sorry.'

'It's fine. I'm up.'

'I just wanted to check in.'

'See if I've made any progress?'

'Well, I mean, not to put too fine a point on it, but our future plans for global domination are kind of riding on it…'

Jane smiled, collapsing down onto the sofa, wondering at the strange sense of disloyalty that was filling her mouth with acid. 'I met him,' she answered, fingers pulling at some fluff on her robe.

Lottie let out a low whistle. 'You only flew in today. That was fast.'

'I went to that bar.'

'And he was there?'

'Yep.'

'Let me guess... He fell at your feet and begged to kiss them?'

Jane rolled her eyes, but the gesture lacked acerbity, because her pulse was throbbing, and her insides were squirming. One touch had ignited her, body and soul. 'No, sadly,' she said, the words sounding foreign to her own ears.

But Lottie didn't appear to notice. 'So, what's the plan?'

'Plan?'

'I presume you have one?'

'Well, he has my number,' she said, and then, sitting a little straighter, 'and I have his.'

'Excellent. You're a genius.'

'Well, we'll see. I get the feeling I'm biting off way more than I can chew.'

'In what way?'

Something twisted in her abdomen. She stood up, pacing, a strange energy making it impossible to sit still. 'He's every bit the practiced flirt, just like we thought.'

'No kidding. You saw the same photos I did, right? A different woman every week?'

'At least,' Jane snorted. 'Maybe even every night. He seemed pretty well known at the bar.'

'I'll just bet he did.' The condemnation in Lottie's voice was pronounced. 'What else?'

'What do you want to know?' Jane asked, ignoring the sense of guilt and focusing on her best friend.

'Nothing,' Lottie responded then with a sigh. 'And everything. He's my half-brother. Does he look like me?'

'No. You know that—you've seen as many pictures as

I have. You're the spitting image of your mother. Apart from your love of coffee and history, I can't imagine you as being half Greek.'

'I like ouzo, too,' Lottie said with a laugh, reminding Jane of the first night they'd gotten properly drunk. That time, they'd broken into the groundskeepers' hut and swiped what they thought was vodka and turned out to be the aniseed Greek spirit. After the first awful taste, they had been undeterred.

'How's your Operation Find a Husband going?' Jane changed the subject with relief and settled back on the couch to listen as Lottie recounted what could only be described as the first date from hell, all the while her naughty imagination kept trying to draw her back to the bar, to Zeus Papandreo and the magic of his touch...

At first, she didn't hear the ringing of her phone, because she was in the middle of a huge crowd of summer tourists, all marvelling at the ancient beauty that was the Acropolis. Beside her, an American family had been debating the architectural merits. Their teenage son had seemed to have a lot to say on the subject, and his parents had been content to let him drone on, and on and on, while their youngest child, a little girl of about seven or eight, devoured a huge ice lolly.

Hot and a little sweaty, Jane was looking at the nearly finished treat with undisguised jealousy when the girl reached out and pointed towards Jane's bag. 'You're ringing,' she said in a broad accent.

Jane blinked, tearing her gaze from the little girl's ice lolly to her face, which was smiling sweetly.

'Oh, right.' She looked across to find that even the teenager had stopped talking, and the parents were looking at her expectantly, too. She realised she was standing very close to their group, almost as if she wanted to be adopted in by them.

She stepped back quickly, smiled curtly then turned away, diving into her bag to remove the phone. In a fit of irritation—self-directed, because she'd been thinking about Zeus and acting like a twit—she answered the phone. Only to hear his voice, coming down the line, dark and somehow every bit as hot as the summer day.

'Jane,' he drawled, the simple word almost indecent. She quickly pulled away from the thrum of people, as much as she could, trying to find somewhere quiet to have this conversation.

'I'm sorry, who's this?' She couldn't resist teasing.

She could practically hear him smirk down the phone. 'We met last night, at the bar.'

'Right. Zoro?'

Now he laughed and she smiled, secure in the knowledge that he couldn't see her, so he wouldn't see how she sort of liked sparring with him.

'Are you free tonight?' he asked, barely a moment later.

She bit into her lower lip. For the sake of self-preservation, she should run a mile. She should tell him 'no,' that she was busy. That was exactly what Jane Fisher would have done, if left up to her own devices. But this was for Lottie. They had a plan, and it was up to Jane to play her part.

'I might be able to move some things in my busy holidaymaker schedule around, depending on what you're suggesting.'

'I'm glad to hear it,' he said, then softly, 'How does dinner sound?'

She expelled a breath of relief. Dinner was fine. Dinner was *out*. In public. No chance of him getting the wrong idea if they were seated across from one another in a busy restaurant.

'Great,' she rushed, trying to remember she should sound delighted and not as though she were heading to the gallows.

'Text me your address and I'll pick you up at eight.'

She bit into her lip. 'I'm at a hotel. I'll get a car to the restaurant.'

Silence. He didn't like being contradicted, she could tell. Well, tough. Jane intended to stay firmly in control of this situation, no matter what. Control was her defence against the dark ravages of her past; control was her salvation.

'What's the matter, Jane?' he asked, but his voice was teasing now, as though he was making fun of her. 'Are you afraid that if I come to your hotel we might decide *not* to go out, after all?'

That was precisely her fear, she admitted to herself. New fears of how much she wanted him, and old fears of being hurt and taken advantage of. Of sacrificing the control she'd fought so hard for.

'Of course not,' she muttered, looking around to make sure she was still alone, a little way off the beaten tourist track. 'But it's not the nineteen fifties. I'm more than capable of making my own way to you.'

She waited for him to argue and wondered how long she'd hold her steel for, but then he simply said, 'Okay. I'll text you the restaurant. See you at eight, Jane.'

She let out a breath of relief.

'And Jane?'

Her heart skipped a beat.

'I'm looking forward to seeing you again.' He disconnected the call, and Jane closed her eyes on a rush of awareness and a growing sense of panic.

She had about five hours to talk some sense into herself and retrain her body so that it wouldn't practically melt whenever he was nearby. Five hours to remind herself that the only reason she was seeing this man—this man she hated on behalf of her best friend and womankind everywhere—was because of the horribly old-fashioned term of inheritance. This meant the world to Lottie, and there was no way Jane was going to let her down. Not after everything she'd already been denied in her life. Jane had her back and always would. She just wished she could stop fantasising about Zeus!

Five minutes after eight, she strode into the restaurant in yet another dress she'd borrowed, this time from her mother's wardrobe. It was a couture dress from a few summers ago, meaning her mother had long since forgotten it existed and wouldn't miss it. A vibrant pink, with slender straps, it clung to the torso then flared at the hips in a skirt that fell to just beneath the knees in a classic prom dress silhouette. But there was something risqué about the dress and the way the back hung low, revealing the line of her spine to just above the curve of her bottom.

She'd teamed it with flats tonight. Even for Lottie and this scheme, she couldn't force her feet into another pair of high heels. Not after she'd walked all over Athens and was still recovering from a dose of pinch-toe-itis courtesy of the night before.

'This way, madam,' a waiter said with a deferential bow when she told him her name.

He led her through the restaurant, past the incredible windows that showed views towards the Acropolis, towards yet another room, this time small enough for one table, and with a sheer curtain hanging across the doorway.

Her heart plunged.

She'd been hoping to sit across from him in a crowded restaurant, not to be in yet another out of the way table like this, with the magic of Athens glittering in the background. They had their own private window, though she supposed, if it was any consolation, the view was hardly likely to get more than a second glance from Jane, given that Zeus was standing up to greet her.

'Jane,' he said, crossing towards her, ignoring the waiter, who faded into the background. She swallowed, but her mouth was inexplicably dry and there was nothing she could do to moisten it. He took her hands in his, held them for a moment then lifted one to his lips. Her stomach dropped to her toes; her insides squeezed with recognition.

'Zeus,' she said, trying to focus. Trying to remember how she needed to act—for Lottie—but also for herself.

'Thank you for meeting me.'

She arched a brow then gestured towards the window,

glad to wrestle back control of her hand. 'You promised to show me the sights. You weren't lying.'

'I never lie,' he said, and guilt coloured Jane's face. She *wasn't* lying to him, though, just by omitting her connection with his family and her reason for being here. He hadn't asked; she was under no obligation to volunteer the information. He put a hand on her hip then, drawing her closer to him, and he kissed her cheek in a manner that was somehow so much more intimate than anything they'd done the night before. A shiver ran the length of her spine.

'I—' she whispered, voice husky. 'I need to tell you something,' she said, pulling away so she could see his face. And the importance of this moment slammed into her. The knowledge that what she told him might ruin Lottie's plan—but that it had to be done. She couldn't keep doing this without putting some guardrails in place; it was too dangerous for Jane. Too hard for her.

His eyes bore into hers and he nodded without making any effort to put some distance between them.

'Last night—what happened in the bar—'

'I thought we discussed this already.'

'No, you decreed I shouldn't explain, but that's not good enough. I have to.'

Amusement sculpted his lips and lifted his brows. 'I decreed?'

'Yes. You're very bossy, you know,' she said with a semi-apologetic grimace.

'I have been told that before.'

'I'm not surprised.'

'Not often so gently, either,' he added, and one side

of her lips tugged upwards in a smile. 'Go on, Jane. Explain whatever it is you would like to say.' He pressed a finger beneath her chin, though, lifting her gaze to his. 'Though I do not consider anything requires an explanation. As I said last night, I felt it, too.'

'You felt what, exactly?'

His eyes flared for a moment and then he pulled her closer, holding her against his body, stroking the naked flesh of her back. 'Desire.'

Yes, desire. It had been a potent force between them, something she'd never really experienced. Not like that—a freight train, rushing headlong towards her. 'Be that as it may,' she said, the conversation becoming almost impossible to focus on when faced with the evidence of the attraction that was flaring between them, particularly from his growing hardness. She closed her eyes, praying for strength. She had to walk a fine line here to keep him interested without selling her soul to the devil. Lottie wouldn't want that, and it was a bridge too far for Jane. This was not, and had never been, about sex. 'I need to be honest with you about my... What I want.'

'I would dearly like to hear all about what you want,' he said, dropping his mouth to the curve of her neck and kissing it, so she groaned and shifted her head to grant him more access. Did she really have to do this? Of course she did. A man like Zeus undoubtedly had relationships that included sex. A lot of sex. And after last night, he probably presumed she was like any of his other conquests; but Jane wasn't. This could only continue if he understood that she needed to go slow.

To be in control. And yet, she angsted back and forth over the necessity of telling him, because a part of her wanted him to see her like any other woman, to kiss her and touch her and possibly even make love to her, because maybe then she could reclaim that part of herself that had been burned by Steven beyond—she'd always thought—repair.

'I'm celibate,' she blurted out, tired of the argument going on in her mind, placing a hand on his chest, needing some space, and sanity, to return.

'Celibate?' He arched a brow enquiringly, as though he'd never heard the word.

'I don't sleep with people.'

'You don't, or you haven't?'

'I haven't, for a very long time,' she admitted, pushing Steven out of her mind with difficulty. 'And I don't intend for that to change anytime soon.'

'I see,' he said when it was clear he didn't. 'Why?'

'I decided I would wait until I was in a committed relationship. With someone I love. And trust.' She lifted one bare shoulder. 'I don't necessarily mean I'm waiting until I get married, but at least…engaged,' she responded. And the moment she told him that—which was the truth, from the bottom of her heart—she realised how a man in his situation might take it.

As an easy way to tick several boxes, all at once.

And her heart began to race at what she'd just unintentionally done.

If she were more Machiavellian, she might have seen it as a masterstroke, but for Jane, it felt as though she was being even more dishonest now. Devious and manipulative.

But he was listening to her with that intelligent, assessing dark gaze, studying her in a way that made her want to squeeze her eyes shut and run a mile, because she feared he saw so much more than she wanted him to.

'I just didn't want you to think, because of last night, that dinner would be a prelude to...you know. Me going home with you.' She took a step back with difficulty, her whole body flushing with cold at the absence of touch. 'If you want me to leave—'

'Leave?' he interrupted, frowning, as though she'd suggested she might grow another head from her hip. 'Why would I want you to leave?'

'Because I know what you're like. What men *like* you are like,' she amended quickly, because she wasn't supposed to know anything about Zeus. 'And I don't want to waste your time.'

'*Agape*, there is not a chance on earth of you doing that. Sit. Tell me more about yourself, starting with your last name.'

CHAPTER FOUR

It was the one thing she could have said to drive him to the breaking point. If there was one thing Zeus loved as much as he hated an ultimatum, it was a challenge, and here was the most beautiful, sensual woman Zeus had ever met, a woman who had had the rare power of keeping him from sleep the night before, so tormented had his dreams been, telling him that she was off-limits.

It was like a red rag to a bull.

But it was something more than that, too.

It's not like I'm waiting until I'm married...

Only, what if she did? What if she waited until she was married, and she just so happened to marry *him*?

He needed a wife. He needed a wife *quickly*, and if last night had proven anything, it was that things between them had the power to move swiftly—faster than either of them had really expected. He thought of Philomena and his insides were cold, despite the fact he knew she was the smart choice.

Jane wasn't marriage material.

No, that wasn't accurate.

He couldn't marry someone like Jane. She was dangerous. Threatening. Because with Jane, there was a risk he might come to want more—that he might actually care about her more than in a sensible, rational, platonic way. Even the way her lip had trembled a little as she'd confessed her celibacy had triggered a long-suppressed protective instinct, reminding him of how he'd felt as a young boy who'd desperately wanted to fix his mother, but couldn't.

Zeus had grappled with that impotence and decided the only antidote to it was strength. Control. Making sure he was in charge of every element of his life. With Philomena, he could imagine that. It was easy. He liked and respected her, she was intelligent and interesting, but he could never imagine becoming addicted to her.

Whereas Jane... His eyes shifted to her face just as she pursed her lips together, almost as if she were nervous, and his stomach twisted.

'What do you do, Jane?'

'Do?'

'For work.'

'Right.' She blinked those wide-set blue eyes, as if he'd dragged her back into the present from some absorbing thought or other. 'I'm a lawyer.'

He tilted his head, thoughtfully.

'That is to say, I have my law degree and was admitted to the bar, but I actually work in the not-for-profit sector.'

'Charities?' he asked, for some reason not surprised. Despite her almost excessive beauty and confidence, there was something vulnerable and sweet about her, too. He could imagine her caring a little too much—the opposite of him, then.

She nodded, and her blond hair, which she'd styled in loose, voluminous waves, bobbed around her face, so he itched to reach out and touch it. To touch her. *I'm celibate.* The words chased around and around in his mind, making him wonder *why*. Clearly, it wasn't a lack of sensual need and desire—he'd felt that flare between them the night before, and her attraction to him had been as unmistakable as his own.

'Which sector?'

'Mostly, I deal with homelessness, though I've just come off a maternity contract working for people leaving domestic violence. We helped get them set up in shelters and whatever else was needed. Oftentimes, these people are leaving with absolutely nothing, so it involves sourcing clothes, computers, new phones and phone numbers so they can apply for jobs, everything.'

He leaned closer, focusing on her with razor-sharp intensity. 'Did you always want to work in charities?'

She tilted her head to the side thoughtfully. 'I guess so.'

'And the law degree was the best way to do that?'

'Actually, I tend to work on the legal side of these foundations, so yes.' She nodded. 'But also—'

He waited for her to continue, wondering at the slight pause, the flushing of her cheeks. She sipped her champagne then leaned forward, mirroring his body language. And when she shifted, her legs moved, too, so her knees brushed against his and he felt a tightening in every cell of his body.

I'm celibate.

'I guess you could say I'm also in the family business.'

'Your parents are lawyers?'

'My father is,' she said with a wave of her delicate, fine-boned hand. Her skin was so flawless, like honey and caramel all melted together.

'In the same sector?'

'Human rights. Edward Fisher. You might have heard of him.'

'Edward Fisher is your father?'

She nodded once.

'Impressive. He's achieved a lot.'

Her smile was tight. 'Yes.'

'You must be very proud.'

'Must I?' She sighed then. 'Sorry, we're not close, but yes, I'm proud of the work he's done.'

Fascinating. Dangerous. Zeus knew he should walk away. Make up an excuse, leave, just like he'd done the night before, then delete her number. Change his if he had to. Because Jane was the last woman he should be spending time with at this point of his life. Right now, when it was imperative that he make the smart decision and marry someone who would be right for him, he couldn't afford to waste time with a woman who had the potential to scuttle all his plans.

Except...it was just dinner. He could spend some time with Jane, see where it went. Philomena had been his friend for a long time; she wasn't going anywhere. If he decided to suggest marriage to her, he could do that in a week, a fortnight, a month. In the meantime, he was free to do what he wanted, just as he always had.

But the sooner you're married, the better, a voice in his head chided him. Then, he could set aside the worry about inheriting the company. He could formalise his ownership, and his father's indiscretion would lose any power to hurt him.

A muscle throbbed in his jaw as he contemplated the deep betrayal of his father's affair, the shifting of the man from the pedestal upon which Zeus had held him. He'd thought they were united in their desire to protect Anna Maria Papandreo. To love her and keep her safe and happy. But all the while, Aristotle had been sleeping around behind her back.

Anger flooded Zeus, so for a moment he almost forgot where he was.

'Zeus?' Jane reached across the table and put her hand on his. 'Are you okay?'

He laughed, but it was a forced, brittle sound. 'I'm fine.'

'Look, if you want to go,' she said with a lift of one of those delightful, bare shoulders, 'I'll understand. I know I'm not what I seem.'

He considered that carefully. 'What do you think you seem like?'

She gestured to her hair first. 'I think guys see the blond hair, my figure, and decide I'm some kind of sex kitten, ready to leap into bed.'

'You're very beautiful,' he said, rather than admit that his first thought upon seeing her had been wondering how quickly he could get her from the bar to his home and naked on his sheets.

Unlike a lot of women he knew, she didn't seem flattered by that. If anything, her expression tightened to one of disappointment and when she said, 'thank you,' it was through gritted teeth. There was more here than she was telling him. More he wanted to understand, because understanding things was one of Zeus's core business strategies. Whenever they'd taken over another company, he'd spent the first month simply observing. Seeing how it ran. Where were the problems? What were the strengths? While it would have been easy to rush in like a bull at a gate with his own ideas and thoughts, he'd have risked missing something important.

'Tell me what happened,' he invited, leaning back in his chair but kicking his legs forward, so they were placed on either side of hers. Jane's eyes widened and heat flared in his gaze; he felt it, too. Desire. A rush of it, wrapping around them like a cocoon, but nothing so comfortable or soporific. No, this was a wild, flagrant cataclysm of animalistic wants, which made it all the more imperative for him to understand why she needed to fight this.

'With my father?' she asked, and he suspected she was deliberately misunderstanding him.

'With your celibacy.'

'Oh.' She glanced down at her drink, and at that moment, the curtain swished open and a waiter walked in. Zeus could have strangled the man, though of course, the intrusion wasn't exactly his fault. Nor was it unexpected. They were at a restaurant; they had to order food. That was how it worked.

'Good evening. Do you have any questions about the menu?'

'I haven't even looked,' Jane murmured.

Zeus fixed the waiter with a stare. 'What does the chef recommend?'

The waiter reeled off a few dishes; Zeus turned to Jane. 'Any problems with that?'

She shook her head and this time, when her blond hair bounced around her angelic face, it released a hint of her fragrance, vanilla and cherries, so his gut clenched. He turned to the waiter to tell him to bring the chef's recommendations and caught the look of undisguised admiration on the other man's face as he also stared at Jane.

Something twisted sharply in Zeus's gut, and not just at the waiter's lack of professionalism. Jealousy. Protectiveness. Emotions that should have made him run a mile, rather than sitting there, waiting impatiently for them to be left alone.

'That's all.' He dismissed the waiter curtly and caught the other man's cheeks darken with a hint of embarrassment. Zeus turned back to Jane.

When they were alone again, she arched a brow and smiled at him. That smile that seemed to filter all the light from all the world and beam it across the room.

'You sound cross.'

He shook his head once. 'I'm not.'

'Not with me,' she said, then lifted her shoulders again. 'Or jealous?'

Was he that transparent? And how bad was that? The fact that he was being so exposed to this woman, when usually he was a closed book. Warning sirens were blaring but he didn't seem capable of heeding them.

'You just told me you don't like being objectified and then he walked in and couldn't stop staring.'

'Isn't that a little like the pot calling the kettle black?'

He didn't like it, but she was right. The night before, he'd seen little beyond her obvious physical beauty. Just like the other men at the bar who'd been ogling her.

'It's fine,' she said, shaking her head. 'I went through a phase where I tried very hard to escape notice, but I got sick of it. It's not my problem if the world views me a certain way. But in terms of men, it's important to be honest. I wouldn't want to lead you on...'

'So, you do date?'

She paled visibly. 'I—'

It would have been kind to let her off the hook. To change the subject to something less important and personal. But Zeus was driven by a selfish need to understand her better, and so he sat silently, staring at her, waiting.

'Yes, I've dated,' she said, biting into that full, lower lip. 'But not seriously. Not since— Not in a while.'

'Something happened,' he said, sure now that he was right, 'to cause you to avoid men.'

She swallowed, her throat shifting visibly. 'Yes.' She toyed with the stem of her champagne flute, then glanced across at him uncertainly. 'I—had what you could call a bad experience. I decided to be very careful after that.'

'You weren't careful before?'

'I was naive,' she muttered. 'And far too trusting.'

He resisted the urge to point out that trusting anyone was a fool's mistake; she didn't seem to need to hear that from him. 'And someone hurt you.'

She flinched, glancing down at her drink. Until that

moment, he'd presumed she meant emotionally, but there was something about the strength of her reaction that thundered all the breath from his body, as he imagined that the hurt she was referencing might, in fact, have been physical.

'Jane...' He chose his words with care, ignoring his own self-preservation instincts, which were still imploring him to run a mile from this woman. 'You don't have to answer this...' He reached out and put his hand on hers lightly, stroking the back of it. 'Are we talking about an abusive relationship?'

Her eyes were saucer-wide when they met his, and to Zeus's relief, she shook her head, hair cascading around her shoulders. But then she looked down at the table once more and it felt as though a noose were tightening about his neck. Because she was hiding something. Lying to him. He knew it. He could tell. Something very bad had happened to her, and just the thought of that made Zeus's blood boil. He stood then, every cell in his body reverberating in rejection of what he was contemplating, as he came to crouch at her side so he could be closer to her, closer to her eye level.

'Listen to me,' he said, one hand on her thigh. She stared at him, eyes wide, lips parted. 'I am not going to pressure you. Not to tell me what you don't want to tell me, and not to do anything you're not comfortable with.' He stroked her thigh gently, saw the moment her pupils dilated, and heat flushed her cheeks. 'But sex, between two consenting adults, is a beautiful, special thing. Not to mention a hell of a lot of fun.' He knelt so he could brush his lips over hers. 'If you've had a traumatic experience in the past, it's natural that you'd want to run from it, that you'd want to avoid situations that might be a repeat of that.' He stroked her cheek, wondering at this strong protective instinct, at the way this woman he'd just met seemed to be the centre of his universe all of a sudden. 'I will never hurt you. I will never push you to do something you're not comfortable with. And I will always, always listen to you. You're in charge.'

Her eyes widened and she nodded, but it was a jerk, a pulse of her head, and he had no idea whether she believed him, or what he was promising. The morning before, he'd woken up with a clear objective, front and centre.

Get married.

To a woman he liked but would never love. To a woman he found attractive but wasn't attracted to. To a woman that couldn't possibly threaten the silo of independence he'd created, very intentionally, around himself.

And instead, he was tumbling headlong, in a way he couldn't fight, into a situation with a woman who had the potential to occupy every single bit of his brain space.

But only if he let her.

Only if he let *this*. Desire, sexual chemistry, these were just part and parcel of being humans in the world. Couldn't he enjoy the physical side of this without letting her get under his skin? She didn't have to threaten anything. He was in control, just like always. Except when it came to sex, because he had an unshakable sense that in that regard, she needed to call the shots. To heal and recover. And he was more than willing to let her use him to get over whatever had happened in her past. After that, he'd get married. To someone else. Someone safe. And the company that meant more than anything to him in the entire world would be, indisputably and irrevocably, his.

Jane's knees were shaking for an entirely different reason now, as she pushed into the ladies' room. Not because she needed to avail herself of the facilities, but because she needed, desperately, space. Having sat opposite Zeus for an entire dinner, legs touching but nothing else, she felt as though her nerves were stretched tighter than a high wire. Her pulse was throbbing and her palms wouldn't stop sweating.

I will never hurt you.

Five words that no man had ever known she needed to hear, an assurance that for some reason, with Zeus, she hadn't needed him to say because she'd *felt* that truth in him, right from the start. The fear she usually felt with the other sex hadn't been there. Not even a little, despite his far greater size and obvious habit of being in command.

With Jane, he was willing to take a backseat. He was willing to let *her* dominate. Because a man with a genuinely strong sense of self wouldn't be intimidated by that. His ego wasn't so fragile that he had to push his will on hers.

But this was all a *disaster*. She wasn't here to be swept away by an attraction to Zeus Papandreo. She was here to tease and tempt him just long enough to stop him from getting married before Lottie could.

What a stupid, stupid idea that had been, she thought with a grimace, staring at her reflection in the mirror. Absent-mindedly, she reached into her purse for some lipstick then carefully reapplied it. How exactly had she thought she'd keep a guy like Zeus interested without sex coming up between them? With witty conversation?

It was not, in the end, a particularly well-thought-out plan. Or maybe the plan had been fine, but meeting Zeus had been her undoing, because she was starting to think he was nothing like she'd suspected.

Had he hurt Lottie? Inadvertently, yes. By being the acknowledged child and heir, the man who'd been raised as a proud Papandreo, he *was* an instrument of pain to Lottie. But it was their shared father, Aristotle, who'd truly wounded Jane's best friend. Zeus wasn't responsible for the choices his father made when he, Zeus, was still just a boy.

Which meant what, exactly? That she was free to flirt with him, after all? To kiss him, touch him, have sex with him? It would achieve the same thing for Lottie. But what about Zeus? Didn't he deserve better than to be used like that?

She dropped her head forward, panic tightening inside her, alongside a growing feeling that she was already in deep, deep water. But maybe the situation with Lottie didn't even have to come into this. She was capable of helping her friend without even having to actively engage in a scheme at all. What was happening with Zeus had morphed into something *genuine*, so it wasn't like she was lying to him, either. She was just… letting this play out. And eventually, she'd go back to the UK, pick up the threads of her own life and Zeus would just be someone in her rear-vision mirror. He'd never need to know her connection to Lottie, and Lottie wouldn't need to know that, far from hating Zeus Papandreo as a loyal best friend should, Jane had actually started to wonder if he mightn't be a genuinely decent person, after all.

CHAPTER FIVE

THE WHOLE DRIVE back to Jane's hotel, neither of them spoke. They sat on opposite sides of the backseat of his car, both very careful to keep a full seat of space between them. But the silence only made Jane more aware. Of his breathing. Of the rustle of his clothes as he shifted in his seat. Of the size of his legs, spread wide, strong and muscular. Athletic.

Athens passed in a blur, the Acropolis a golden beacon visible through the front windscreen, but Jane barely noticed the beauty of the backdrop. Every single atom of her was focused on Zeus. When they'd left the restaurant, he'd offered his driver to take her back to the hotel. Solo. Without him.

Because he'd promised to respect her boundaries, and he was showing her that he meant it. But Jane had demurred, saying that it was silly for the driver to drop her while he caught a cab. 'Can't you just drop me off first?' Their eyes had met and something had fizzed between them, a spark had ignited, and it was still burning.

But Jane knew that it was her decision how long she let it go for. If she wanted, at the hotel, she could turn to Zeus and say good-night and send him on his way.

He wouldn't question it—that was their deal. And that was what she should do, she knew. If only to test him, to make sure he was being honest, when he promised that she was in charge.

It was an assurance, though, she found she didn't need, because for some reason she couldn't explain, Jane trusted him. At least, she trusted him as much as it was possible for her to trust someone. Naturally, there was still a wariness because of what Steven had done to her, and after how much she'd loved and cared for him, but this was different. Zeus was different.

You don't know that, a voice chided.

Was she being just as naive as she'd been back then?

The car pulled to a stop in front of her hotel, and she turned to face him, to find an expression on his face that made her stomach somersault.

'I enjoyed spending time with you, Jane.'

He made no effort to move. True to his word, she thought, heart lifting.

Say good-night and go upstairs.

She glanced at the seat between them, where his tanned hand rested, and bit into her lower lip.

'I did, too,' she half whispered.

'I'd like to see you again.'

She swallowed, her throat dry. 'I—' *Say good-night. Leave. Get out of the car.* 'Would you like to come up for coffee?'

Good Lord. The words tumbled out of her mouth without a skerrick of forethought, almost as if her body had ideas that her brain definitely didn't condone.

'We had coffee at the restaurant,' he pointed out with a wry smile. 'But I'd like to come up, regardless.'

Their eyes met and the spark that had been burning tilted dangerously close to a full-blown explosion. Uncertainty thickened in her gut, but so did desire, and it was not a fair fight. After so long of subduing her sensual needs, the temptation of Zeus was impossible to ignore. He'd stirred something to life inside her just by his presence, and she felt as though it was impossible to fight it.

'Okay,' she said, and nodded slowly, because it was an agreement to so much more than heading upstairs. 'Let's go.'

She'd never noticed how small elevators were before. And it wasn't like the elevators in this fancy five-star hotel were even that small, but with Zeus right beside her, she felt his proximity and heat like a magnet. She glanced up at him as the doors swished closed and he turned, slowly, to regard her with eyes that were shiny dark and mesmerisingly intense. 'Remember, Jane, you're in charge,' he said, voice a low rumble.

'Why do I think you're not used to handing over control?' she asked, her voice strangely airy.

He arched a brow in a way that made her stomach loop in on itself. 'Which floor?'

'Oh, right, the key,' she muttered, reaching into her clutch purse and fumbling a little, because her fingers wouldn't cooperate. He waited patiently, but the longer he waited, the harder it got, because he was so close, and all she could think about was the way they'd kissed the night before, and wondering if they'd kiss again, and wanting, more than anything, for that to be the case.

But what if he did hurt her?

What if she couldn't trust him?

Steven had seemed trustworthy. Steven had always said all the right things, and then he'd treated her like a piece of meat. He'd grown tired of waiting for her to be ready to sleep with him, so he'd made sure it had happened.

What if—?

'Would you like me to do it?' he asked, and she realised she'd stopped fumbling and was staring at the breadth of his chest.

She nodded slowly, holding her clutch out to him. He didn't take the bag but rather reached inside and easily fished out the key card from the side pocket, then took her hand in his and upended it, so he could place the key card there. Rather than letting go, though, he came to stand beside her, his body pressed to hers, and he held her hand still as he guided it towards the pad on the elevator panel and swiped it. Her floor lit up immediately. She expelled a breath of relief—a sense of relief that only seemed to grow when he stayed right there, behind her, one hand wrapped around her wrist, his thumb brushing over her flesh gently.

She wasn't just aware of the sound of his husky breathing now, but of the feel of it, as his chest moved with each exhalation, and the air in the elevator seemed to grow thick and warm. Her whole body was throbbing, like her pulse had become overlarge and was taking over every organ. She wanted to turn around, to be standing *this* close to him, but toe to toe, to feel him, to see him. But she stayed as she was, because she had a feeling they were both out of their depths a little—even Zeus—and she knew that one wrong move would explode the whole situation.

And if it got really out of hand? Would she have any choice but to run a mile from this?

She swallowed past a lump in her throat, and when the doors opened to reveal the plushly carpeted corridor of her hotel level, she released a breath. Of relief, and gratitude.

'This is me,' she said, reluctant to move.

'So I gathered.'

He moved then, extending a hand to keep the doors open, his eyes on her with an emotion she couldn't fathom. 'After you.'

She nodded once, tried to make her legs move, but there was a lack of synergy between her brain and body. Or maybe it was that she was right where she wanted to be—close to Zeus—and so she found herself stuck there.

He held out his other hand to her then, broad and tanned, inviting her to put her own in his. More than a gesture, it was a sign of trust. Of him asking her to trust him, and when she placed her hand in his palm, and he closed his fingers over hers, it was as though she'd agreed.

She hoped she wasn't wrong, that this wasn't all an awful mistake.

They stepped off the elevator together. 'Which way?'

She gestured to the left and they began to walk, hand in hand, towards her door. She paused outside the front of it, then swiped her key, which she was still holding in her other hand.

The door clicked to show that it had unlocked, and Zeus pushed it open, standing where he was but holding it back against the wall, so Jane could enter first. She took a step, then realised he wasn't following.

'I can leave, Jane,' he said, misreading her hesitation. Because she wanted him to come in. She wanted everything to happen between them that the flame and flares seemed to promise *would* happen. But she just didn't know *how* to give in to that. She'd spent so long fighting this part of herself, forcing it down. Or maybe it just hadn't even been an issue, because she'd never met anyone since Steven who'd made her want to try this again. With Zeus, it didn't even feel like a choice.

'No,' she demurred, the word thick with urgency. 'I really do want you to come in. It's just—'

He waited, looking at her in that inquisitive way he had.

'I don't know what happens next,' she said, honestly, shrugging her shoulders. 'It's been a long time, and I'm—'

He reached forward and pressed a finger to her lips. 'We're not sleeping together tonight.'

Her heart sank to her toes and her brows drew inwards as she tried to process that. 'Oh.'

'Not because I don't want to,' he assured her quickly, as though he understood the doubt and uncertainties that had instantly plagued her. 'But because I think you need time to get used to the idea. To make sure it's what you really want.'

Her pulse ratcheted up. 'What if I already know it's what I want?'

His eyes widened and then swept shut, and she somehow just knew that he was fighting a battle of his own—between what he wanted and what he knew he should be doing.

'Then you'll still want it tomorrow night. Or the night after that. We don't have to rush this.'

Which was exactly what *she* should have been saying. Because this was about distracting him from getting engaged—except it wasn't. When she was alone with Zeus, it was about this and only this. Desire, need, want, pleasure. Lottie's plans were the furthest thing from her mind.

She nodded slowly, and only then did he step inside the hotel room. The door clicked shut between them and there they stood, toe to toe, just as she'd wanted to be in the elevator.

Her own breathing was rushed, her chest moving rapidly, so she was aware of the way her dress tightened across her breasts.

'This dress,' he muttered, reaching behind her and pressing a finger to her exposed back, 'should be illegal.'

She laughed softly, pleasure trilling in her veins. 'You like it?'

He grimaced. 'A little too much.'

'That's a shame. I was thinking of getting changed out of it.'

'Jane,' his voice held a warning.

She held one hand up between them, to reassure him. 'It's a beautiful dress. It's just not that comfortable.' She met and held his gaze. 'I want to take it slowly, too, Zeus. I need that. I just—still want to—' She tapered off, not sure how to express what she was feeling.

'Do something?' he prompted, putting his hands on her hips and holding her there. She shivered from desire, and in the back of her mind, she marvelled at how calm she felt. Where usually being alone with a man who was attracted to her flooded her veins with fear, she felt nothing like that now.

She nodded. 'So, maybe you could help me get changed?' she prompted, knowing that she was inviting them both to play with fire, and not caring.

His eyes flared and then he moved his hands lower, gliding them over the swell of her hips to her thighs, bunching the delicate fabric as he went. 'I did say you were in charge, didn't I?' he murmured, reaching the hem and holding it in his fists.

Pulse in her throat, she nodded again.

Slowly, oh, so painstakingly slowly, he lifted the dress upwards. Past her thighs, over her bottom to her waist, where he paused, eyes on hers the whole time, as if reading her, wanting reassurance that she was still okay with this. He was taking his promise very, very seriously, and the proof of that exploded the last vestiges of her doubt.

Zeus wasn't Steven.

Zeus was a man who could have any woman he wanted; he didn't need to force himself on some drunk teenager. He had principles and confidence; he was different to Steven in every way.

She lifted her hands over her head in a silent invitation—and insistence—that he keep going. He did.

Slowly, though, so slowly she wanted to scream, his fingers brushing her sides as he pushed the dress towards her breasts and then over them. The contrast between the warmth of his touch and the cool of the air around them made the hair on her arms stand on end. The fabric was soft and it rustled against her ears when he finally pulled it over her head, then dropped it to the floor at their sides with a hiss from between his teeth.

'Holy mother of God,' he groaned, stepping forward and pressing their bodies together, hers naked except for a flimsy pair of lace briefs. 'You are exquisite.'

But she didn't want to hear that. She didn't care about physical beauty, and she didn't particularly want it to be what he saw in her, either.

She lifted up onto the tips of her toes and her eyes held his as she slowly, hungrily, sought his mouth with her own. And groaned. In the bar, he'd kissed her as though she were a woman he desired, but here, alone in her hotel room, with her virtually naked, he kissed her as though she were an *objet d'art* that he desperately wanted to explore. His lips separated hers, his tongue danced against hers, his mouth was warm, like his fingers, and yet he was careful not to overwhelm her. Even when she wanted to be overwhelmed.

Frustration stretched inside her. She didn't want him to treat her like a fragile vase; she wanted to be treated like a red-blooded woman, thick with desire and needs that only he could assuage.

'Touch me,' she demanded, remembering the skill he'd shown in the bar the previous night. Before he'd known that she'd been hurt, that she was, in so many ways, fragile and vulnerable. 'Show me what I've been missing.'

He groaned into her mouth and she felt it again—that duality of Zeus. What he wanted, and what he thought he should be. Well, she was giving him permission to go with the former. He knew she had boundaries. He was the one who'd acknowledged those boundaries by laying it out: they weren't going to have sex tonight. But that didn't mean they couldn't do other things.

'I'm begging you,' she said against his mouth. 'Touch me. Make me feel like you did last night. Please.'

And on that last, desperate plea, his body shuddered and something inside him seemed to snap, because he dropped to his knees then, his hands on her hips shifting to the lace of her panties and loosening them, pulling them down her legs, so she could step out of them. At the same time she kicked her shoes off and stood before him completely undressed.

One of his hands came behind her and clasped over her rear, holding her where she was as his mouth teased the sensitive flesh at the top of her legs, flicking her inner thigh until she was trembling and flushed with heat, and then he was pushing her backwards, towards the wall, as if he somehow understood that she needed more support. One of his hands came between her legs, spreading them wider, and then his mouth was on her sex, his tongue flicking her, teasing her, making her cry out because she'd never been kissed like this before. She knew oral sex was a thing, but it was not something she'd ever imagined she would want to have done to her, nor that it could feel this good.

In fact, she hadn't known *anything* could feel this good. Her hands tore through his hair as madness seemed to saturate her soul, and then his fingers were there, too, pressing against her clitoris, moving faster, while his mouth shifted to the flatness of her stomach, kissing, tasting, and then his fingers were inside her and her hips were bucking hard as the waves of pleasure he'd built became almost too much to bear.

'Zeus,' she cried his name, then swore in an uncharacteristic gesture, because she was completely overwhelmed. He glanced up at her with a question in his eyes and she nodded her reassurance. 'Please, don't stop,' she groaned, half laughed, then cried out again as he returned his mouth to her, his fingers still buried in her depths, so the sensory overload was immense.

'I'm—I feel—I'm—' But she couldn't explain what was happening to her; she only knew that it was the best feeling in the world. Her whole body trembled and tingled, her nipples seemed to throb and ache, her knees were weak, her body was sheened in perspiration, and just the sight of him, between her legs, was sending her tumbling down a rabbit hole that she wondered if she'd ever find her way out of. Her body exploded with an all-consuming ferocity, a feeling she wanted to bottle and keep forever. Waves of it kept washing over her until she couldn't think straight, and her breathing was rushed and her voice hoarse. She stood there, grateful beyond words for the support of the wall, and the way his hand was clamped at her hip to stop her from sliding sideways. Her breathing was rushed, as though she'd run a marathon.

He stood, and before she could regain her breath, he was kissing her. Not slowly and inquisitively this time, not as though she were something fragile he was afraid of breaking, but with all the hunger and passion he'd just stirred. Kissing her as though she were the meaning to everything on this earth. Lifting her as though she weighed nothing, cradling her against his chest, kissing her still as he strode, long and confident, through the hotel room corridor and deeper into her suite. The bedroom was to the right; he found it easily and placed her on the bed but didn't leave.

Oh, no.

He came down on top of her, kissing her, so his weight was on her and for a moment, a moment that shocked her because it had no place here, with them, an old feeling of suffocating and being helpless and afraid, came back, so she froze. He must have perceived her stillness, because he stopped kissing her immediately and pushed up onto his elbows, relieving her of his weight.

Disappointment was sharper than relief, because Zeus wasn't Steven, and this was not that night.

He stroked her cheek, and her heart twisted. 'Okay?'

She nodded.

He arched a brow, as if he didn't believe her.

'Really,' she promised. She pushed up onto her elbows, so she could kiss him again, and this time, when he relaxed down on top of her, she was capable only of enjoying the pleasure of their bodies being melded together like this, the heat of him, the strength of him. Her hands roamed his back, the curve of his toned bottom, her nails digging in there, before she crept her hands higher and pulled his shirt from his waistband so that her fingertips could connect with the bare flesh of his back.

He hissed again and pushed away from her, this time fully off the bed, jackknifing away from Jane as though she'd detonated a bomb between them.

'What is it?' she asked, on her elbows once more so she could see him better. And she could *see*, very clearly, how turned on he was by what they'd been doing.

'Don't do that.'

'What?' Her eyes widened in surprise. Had she done something wrong?

'I'm holding on by a thread,' he muttered apologetically. 'When you touch me…'

'Oh.' Pleasure made her smile. 'I'm glad to hear I'm not alone in that department.'

He grimaced. 'You said you wanted coffee?'

'Coffee?' She pulled a face. 'Believe me, that's the last thing on my mind.'

'A cold shower?'

She laughed. 'Nope.'

'Jane—'

'Come here.' She patted the bed beside her, but he stayed where he was. 'What if,' she said, thinking aloud, 'I promise not to touch you?'

His eyes flared.

'But you can touch me,' she said slowly, seductively. 'Anywhere, any way you want to.'

His Adam's apple throbbed.

'No sex,' she reiterated, because he was right: that was a step she wanted to think about. And be completely sober for. Even though she'd only had two glasses of bubbles with dinner, her experience with Steven had been traumatising enough to know she would only ever make that choice when she could 100 percent trust her judgement.

'I've never met anyone like you,' he said, but to her immense relief he began to stride back towards the bed—and her.

'I think that might be mutual,' she confessed, swallowing a sigh as he sat beside her and then kissed her hard, fast and hungrily, just how she wanted him to be with her.

CHAPTER SIX

FOR THE SECOND night in a row, Zeus couldn't sleep. It had been hard enough the night before, when they'd kissed in the bar, but after everything that had happened between them in her hotel—and what specifically *hadn't* happened—he had a raging hard-on and an insatiable need for a woman he hadn't even known for seventy-two hours.

Right when he needed to be his most pragmatic self, it was like the universe, or fates, had conspired to send him a vixen—a woman who pushed *all* of his buttons. Sexy, beautiful, intelligent and vulnerable, so that he felt those warrior instincts he'd honed during his mother's cancer fight burst back to life. Even when he'd told himself he'd never care enough about another human to want to fight their battles for them. Even when he knew the cost of caring too deeply for anyone.

As the sun began to creep towards the cityscape, Zeus gave up on even attempting to sleep, slipped into a pair of shorts, a T-shirt and some joggers and let himself out of his mansion. Running had long been a balm to his busy mind, a way to not only calm his thoughts but, more importantly, to also bring order to them.

It wasn't like being attracted to a woman was new. Zeus had made an artform out of the three-night stand. One night was too short—he liked to get to know the women he slept with. Anything more than three nights was way too long, because he didn't like to risk caring too much about them.

Until Jane, he'd never found it hard to live by that creed.

He supposed he bored easily. Or perhaps the women he'd been dating had been wrong for him, in terms of being able to hold his attention. Except, wasn't that exactly what he'd been aiming for? To be able to enjoy a woman's company for a brief while, then walk away without a backwards glance?

Something crept up his spine and left the hairs on the back of his neck standing on end, because when he imagined walking away from Jane, he didn't feel as though it would be easy, and he didn't feel as though he'd be prepared to do it in two nights' time. Which surely gave him all the more reason to do precisely that.

She was dangerous to him—he'd thought that before. He'd known it from their first meeting. She was *too* beautiful, too sexy, too alluring, too vulnerable, too everything, and suddenly, all of Zeus's carefully laid boundaries were being pulled at and weakened by a woman he knew virtually nothing about.

Except, he did know that she wasn't planning to be in Athens long-term. He did know that she was as committed to her career as he was to his. And he did know that getting married was as imperative now as it had been since his father told him about his half-sister.

Every day without a marriage licence being procured was a day closer to the risk of losing the company. Was he seriously willing to take the chance of waking up one day to find that he was no longer in the box seat to inherit the Papandreo Group? Of course not. The business was so much more than just a business to Zeus; it had to remain his.

Unless there was a way he could meet his half-sister, he thought, pausing midstride and standing still, hands on hips, breath rushed, as he stared out at the dawn-lit city.

He didn't *want* to meet her. He didn't want to come face-to-face with the evidence of his father's failings. But maybe he could offer her something to get rid of the threat altogether. Money. Enough money to make her realise that the company itself wouldn't be worth fighting for.

Except, what fool would take a lump sum, rather than the ongoing cash cow of the Papandreo Group? Was it worth making the offer, on the basis she *might* accept? Or did it risk exposing to her how badly he wanted to retain his position? And once she knew that, might she fight harder to secure the windfall she'd only just learned about?

He made a gruff sound of irritation, wishing he knew *something* about the woman his father had conceived behind his mother's back and realising, belatedly, that he *could* find out a little more about her. His skin slicked with something like distaste. He was not a man who would ordinarily engage the services of a private investigator, but surely, this was a time for desperate measures. To protect his business, his family's legacy and empire, to do the right thing for people who couldn't see clearly enough to do it for themselves, he thought, breaking into a run once more.

Yes, he committed to the idea, as he turned the corner towards his home, five miles later. He would hire a detective, he would find out more about what he was dealing with and then, if necessary, he'd explain the situation to Philomena and ask if she'd be willing to be his wife of convenience.

Jane would be, by then, a moot point, because she would have to be. Unlike his father, Zeus intended to take his marriage vows seriously, even if that meant turning his back on a woman who had very quickly become the sum total of what he wanted in his day.

Though she felt exhausted, Jane woke early the next morning. There was a restlessness inside her, a sense of impatience, and despite the way Zeus had worshipped her body the night before, Jane had woken up in the early hours wanting *more*. So. Much. More.

Snatches of memories filtered through her mind as she showered, lathering her still-too-sensitive body with a loofah and soap, revelling in the feeling of the water cascading over her head. Afterwards, she contemplated ordering room service—she was also famished—but decided instead to set out on foot and explore more of this city.

To walk.

To burn off her abundance of energy and try to put Zeus out of her mind.

She dressed in a pair of shorts and a singlet top, in preparation for a day that promised to be hot and grabbed a cap on her way out of the hotel room—she had no idea how long she'd be gone for, and her skin had a tendency to fry.

Not two blocks from the hotel, she stopped at a quaint little *kafenio*, with white chairs spilling out onto the street. She ordered her usual oat latte and added a toasted flatbread with saganaki, spinach and eggplant. It arrived steaming hot, and she sat down to enjoy it, content to watch the world pass her by.

It was a sense of contentment that didn't last long.

Last night, in a fog of sensual need, of white-hot lust, she'd thrown herself headlong into the maddening rush of desire. She hadn't allowed herself to dwell on the consequences nor the complications of what they were doing. But as the sun rose and bathed Athens in a glorious golden hue—a colour that somehow seemed to echo the vagaries of time, imprinting this city's ancient presence on Jane—she was forced to see what had happened with all the shock that broad daylight could bring.

She bit into the flatbread, the gooey, melted cheese perfectly salty and dribbling a little from the edge. She wiped it absent-mindedly with her finger, focusing on a man across the street who was stacking newspapers into a vending machine.

After that night with Steven, she'd awoken groggy, hungover and sore all over. Muscles she'd never used before had screamed their complaint as she'd pushed out of the unfamiliar bed and looked around, trying desperately to get her bearings. Bruises across her torso, hickeys on her thigh, only very briefly preceded the onslaught of memories. Awful, awful memories. A feeling of having been totally out of control, unable to properly express what she was feeling and what she wanted—for it to stop.

This was different.

This morning Jane had woken with clarity and recollection. She didn't regret what had happened between her and Zeus, and she wanted *more* of it, and him. But she also needed a clear path forward. A way to do this without betraying her own sense of right and wrong, with regards to her promise to Lottie.

She closed her eyes and inhaled the fragrance of her coffee, wishing that it could somehow, magically, give her the guidance she sought.

Three days ago, she would have sworn that nothing and nobody would ever change what she owed Lottie and what Lottie meant to her. And the same was true this morning, she swore. But entering into an intentionally manipulative flirtation with Zeus Papandreo was so much more complicated now she knew him.

And liked him.

She dropped her head in shame, and her heart began to trot in a rhythm all its own.

Yes, she liked him.

He was nothing like she'd expected. At least, not in the ways that mattered. While he was confident, he wasn't arrogant. He was proud, but not unreasonably so, and he was so much more courteous and considerate than his reputation foreshadowed.

She took another bite of the sandwich, her features a study in misery.

If she told Lottie what was happening, would Lottie understand and perhaps tell her to come home? And then what? Would she just fly away from Zeus without giving him an explanation? And could she even bear to do that? Did she *want* to leave him?

No.

She wanted to stay and explore this to its fullest.

Last night she'd told herself this would be like killing two birds with one stone, only so much happier than killing. She could explore this with Zeus and get Lottie what Lottie wanted, and no one ever had to know how disastrously conflicted she'd felt about it all.

But what about Zeus? What about the business he obviously loved? Could she really live with being an instrument in his losing that? And if not, what did that mean for Lottie? She knew what this meant to her best friend—what it was supposed to mean to both of them.

She groaned, placing the sandwich back on the cardboard tray and gingerly wiping her fingertips together. There was no way to extricate herself from this situation without hurting someone. Lottie or Zeus. Lottie, her best friend of more than a decade, a woman who was more like a sister to her than anything else, clearly should have the biggest stake on her heart. And on her heart, she did. But her obligations? Her conscience?

She picked up her takeaway coffee cup and began to walk, frowning deeply, so she missed the hue of peach and pink that lit the sky as the sun grew higher, missed the purples, too, that reached out like long, magical fingers, directly across the horizon. She walked a long way, down a wide, straight street lined with large, verdant trees. She walked until her body was sheened in perspiration and then pulled her phone out to check the time, only to see several text messages on the front screen.

Lottie's required her attention first. I miss you! X

Guilt brightened the flush in her cheeks. The next message was from her mother.

Are you coming to the races next weekend? We have a box.

Jane rolled her eyes. For a long time, Jane had held little value to her parents, but now, an intelligent graduate who had morphed into a doppelgänger of the elegant Mrs Fisher, Jane was suddenly a worthwhile accessory for certain society events. She clicked out of that message and then, with a fluttering in her chest, tapped into Zeus's.

Can I see you tonight?

Her heart went from fluttering to exploding and she stepped sideways so she could lean against a building for support. Never mind that it was covered in years of dust and grime and Jane was wearing pale clothes. In that moment, she needed help just to stay standing.

She thought about what to respond with. Could he see her? There was nothing she wanted more.

And *that* was the problem.

It was all happening too fast, getting too intense,

starting to *mean* too much. They needed to put the brakes on, slow it all right down, make it more casual, more fun. Maybe then she'd be able to live with herself for intentionally plotting his professional downfall.

She groaned and shook her head, hating what she'd agreed to suddenly.

She clicked out of his text and into Lottie's.

We need to talk. Call me when you're free.

She began to walk once more, her stride long and intent. Coffee finished, she discarded the cup in a nearby wastebin, then turned and looked around, realising that she'd wandered without paying attention and had no idea how to get back to the hotel. She lifted her phone from her pocket and saw another text from Zeus.

No pressure.

Her heart rolled over in her chest.

If only he knew how untrue that was! Jane was under the kind of pressure that could fell a person. She needed to speak to Lottie. She loaded a map up and began to walk towards her hotel, willing her phone to ring, and for it to be her best friend on the other end. Wishing, more than anything, that in speaking to Lottie, she'd somehow know exactly how to proceed.

Zeus was getting used to 'firsts' with Jane, and that afternoon he recognised another one.

It was the first time he'd messaged a woman and not

heard back almost instantly. The first time he'd sent *multiple* messages and had them be ignored.

He vacillated between irritation and concern for the better part of the day. Irritation with himself, and with her. Irritation that he felt completely unlike normal and desperately didn't like it. Irritation with her for the power she somehow wielded over him.

Concern, because last night had been intense. True, they hadn't slept together, but he'd enjoyed stirring her to a fever pitch. He'd revelled in the power he held in that moment over her, to make her whimper and thrash, to make her body explode, and he'd driven her wild again, and again and again, until she was so exhausted she could hardly keep her eyes open. Then, he'd lifted her higher into the bed, covered her with the blankets and kissed her forehead before letting himself, and his rock-hard arousal, out.

Only a promise to himself that he'd see her again soon had allowed him to leave at all. He'd sized up the sofa and considered sleeping there, just so he'd be able to pick up where they'd left off in the morning.

Maybe it was because he was on the brink of making a commitment to someone else. It was possible that the knowledge a marriage was imminent for Zeus was making his brain and body perceive Jane as more special somehow than she really was. But even as he thought that Hail Mary, he knew it was a false hope, because the way he felt for Jane had everything to do with her, and nothing to do with the arcane inheritance surrounding the company.

He stood from his desk angrily and strode across the

expansive office, staring out at the landscape of Athens' central business district. It was a view that usually puffed his chest with pride. He loved this city; he loved his family's contributions to both it and the broader landscape of Greece. He was a Papandreo, and in taking over the running of the company, Zeus was carrying on a proud, important tradition.

Not once had he questioned the righteousness of that.

But his father's stupidity and weakness had put everything in jeopardy. Now guilt was making the older man weak in an even worse way than infidelity: he was being reckless with the business. He was willing to bring in an outsider to run it, never mind her lack of experience and the fact she was his bastard daughter with God only knew who.

Zeus's entire world was shattering, just like it had again and again as a boy, a teenager and finally, for good when his mother had died. Though by then, he'd hardened his heart to her loss, knowing that it was coming, accepting that he was powerless to save her, and that he would not make her pain worse by showing his grief. He wouldn't burden her with that; he was brave, to the end.

Breathing in deeply, so his chest stretched and flooded with air, he turned his back on the view and stalked back to his desk, reaching for his phone. No replies, still.

Grinding his teeth, he picked up his phone to make a call, but not to Jane. If only to prove to himself that he was still in control of his life, that he wasn't as utterly and completely at her beck and call as he feared he might be.

* * *

'Finally,' Jane groaned down the line, sinking into the sumptuous sofa of her hotel suite and staring out at the windows. 'I've been waiting for you to ring.'

'Sorry, I was on a flight.'

'To where?'

'That doesn't matter.' Lottie sounded harried, though. 'Is everything okay?'

'Fine. What's up?'

Jane frowned. 'I—' But now that it came to it, she struggled to find the words. How could she tell her best friend that the man they'd always, always hated was the most deliciously sexy person on earth? And that he also happened to be kind and interesting…? It felt like a betrayal of the highest order, and so she cast about for how to begin.

'Is it Zeus?' Lottie demanded. 'Are you okay?'

'I'm… Yes. Of course. Why?'

Lottie expelled a long breath. 'I just— I've been worrying that maybe I sent you on a quest to the lion's den. I couldn't live with myself if he hurt you, too, Jane.'

Jane squeezed her eyes shut, unsure how to confess that she feared she was the one who would be hurting *everyone* if she wasn't very careful.

'He's not going to hurt me,' she promised, and found the words were spoken with confidence.

'God, I hope not. I wouldn't trust him as far as I could throw him.'

'He's not like we thought, Lottie.'

Silence sparked. A silence that Jane perceived, because she knew Lottie as well as she did herself, was loaded and important.

'Oh?'

Jane bit back a groan. 'He's actually quite...nice.'

Nice! What a weak, watery word to describe Zeus Papandreo.

'At least, he's not the complete piece of work we'd always presumed.'

'I beg your pardon. No one who goes through women like that is *nice*.'

Jane chewed on her lower lip. 'I'm not saying he's perfect—'

'You hardly know him,' Lottie pointed out. 'You've only been in Athens a few nights.'

'I know,' she said, wondering why inwardly she rebelled against that as a concept. Hardly knew him? It didn't seem to come close to describing their relationship. 'I guess I just have a sense for...'

'Listen,' Lottie interrupted. 'Nice or not, he's my sworn enemy, and you're my bestest friend.' Her tone was joking, but Jane didn't smile. 'I want that company, and his father—Aristotle—has given me the perfect way to get it. To rip it out from *both* of them. It's not about Zeus. It's about my mother, what they took from her, took from me. It's about payback. It's about what I deserve.'

A single tear slid down Jane's cheek, because Lottie wasn't wrong, either. Jane knew what the secret affair had done to Lottie's mother, who'd never stopped loving Aristotle, even though she did her best to hide it. 'I know,' she whispered.

'Oh, God, Jane. You're crying. What's happened? Please tell me... I can't bear for you to get hurt.'

'It's just— I want you to have everything you want, Lottie, you know that. But...'

'You don't want to hurt him.'

She squeezed her eyes shut.

'You're too kind,' Lottie groaned. 'Look, he'll get over it. He'll get over you.'

'But not losing the business,' she said, remembering the pride in his features when he spoke of his place in the Papandreo legacy. Only that night, she'd hated him for his pride, because it had been stolen from Lottie. Now? It was intrinsic to him.

She toyed with the fabric hem of her shorts.

'He'll still be worth a stinking fortune,' Lottie pointed out. 'He can rebuild, do something else. He can use the same damned name for all I care.'

Jane swallowed past a bitter lump in her throat. Loyalty to Lottie was her principal duty, but only just.

'Let me put it this way,' Lottie continued. 'What do you think he'll do if he gets married before me?'

Jane stared across the room in silence.

'Do you think he'll give one iota of thought about me?'

Jane scrunched her eyes closed.

'Of course he won't. He'll take his triumph, his ownership of all things Papandreo, and that will be the end of it.' Lottie's voice stung, and Jane understood why. This was about so much more than the company. Lottie had been wronged her whole life by these people, even though Jane couldn't have said with certainty if Zeus had even known about her. The effect was the same. Lottie had grown up believing herself to be a shameful secret, seeing hurt in her mother's face and heart, knowing herself to be, in some way, an instrument of that. And if, or rather when, Zeus married, he would, Jane had no doubt, shut down any legal recourse Lottie had to staking a claim on the business.

'I'll stay for a week,' she said on a soft, tortured sigh. 'One week, to give you a head start. After that, I'm leaving Athens, and Zeus, and I don't ever want to hear his name again, okay?'

'A week?' Lottie groaned but quickly cut herself off. 'A week,' she repeated with much more strength. 'Okay, okay. I can work with that.'

Jane grimaced. 'Lottie...maybe there's a way you can have some of the company, but not all.'

'Are you actually suggesting I compromise with those bastards?'

Jane sighed softly. She had been, but she should have known better. She'd witnessed the hatred Lottie felt for them—up until very recently, Jane had felt it, too.

'No.'

'Look, take care of yourself,' Lottie begged. 'I know I've asked you to do a lot. I know how hard it is for someone like you to be, I guess, kind of ruthless, but for me, can you just *try*?'

She nodded unevenly, then remembered Lottie couldn't see her. 'One week,' she promised, and disconnected the call with a thud in the region of her chest.

One week was a slight head start to Lottie, but not a huge disadvantage to Zeus, either. And it did give her the safety to see him again, without worrying about how to extricate herself. She flicked her phone screen to life and loaded up Zeus's text messages.

How about dinner tonight? I can come to you...

CHAPTER SEVEN

HE'D CHOSEN ANOTHER glamorous restaurant, absolutely packed to the rafters with stunning A-listers, and it was clear that Zeus was well known here. Not because he was Zeus Papandreo, but because he was a regular at places like this, in this scene.

Jane regarded him across their small table, her head tilted slightly to the side, her heart in her throat. Maybe Lottie had been right. Maybe Zeus was just like they'd always thought, and it was Jane who was layering more humanity and decency over him than he actually possessed. But the way he'd kissed her forehead the night before and crept out, rather than trying to push his advantage and hop into bed with her, had been nothing if not chivalrous. Not to mention the way he'd made her feel...

'I have to tell you something,' she blurted out. He leaned closer, eyes boring into hers, making every part of her feel seen and exposed.

'That sounds ominous.' His voice, though, was relaxed. Casual. Easy-going. As though he didn't care, one way or another. About her, or whatever she was about to say. Jane frowned. Was it possible she'd been wrong about the intensity of this? She'd slept with one man, once. She'd been celibate ever since. Suddenly, she'd met someone who made her feel as though her knickers had caught fire; maybe it was the most natural thing in the world that she'd overlay those feelings with something more.

Something more than just casual attraction.

'Oh, it's no big deal.' She tried to mirror his tone. 'I've just had a change of plans. I'm heading home next week.'

Something flashed in his eyes. Something that she could have sworn was an emotion, but what? It didn't last long enough to even try to analyse it; a moment later, he was all suave and in control once more. 'What changed?' Casual enquiry, nothing more.

'A job,' she lied. 'I got an email today, so I'm heading back.'

'Another charity?'

She thought quickly. 'One I've worked at before.' God, she hated lying to him, though. In fact, she hated lying in general, but to Zeus, it felt like an awful betrayal. Still, this was how it had to be. She needed to put an end to this without letting Lottie down completely. A week was the best compromise she could offer.

'Okay,' he replied, nodding. But then his eyes sparked when they met hers, and he leaned across the table. 'Do you get seasick?'

She stared at him, the question coming completely out of left field. 'Erm, not that I know of.'

'What do you say about a week on my yacht, then?'

Her eyes widened. 'What?'

'We can explore the Med, all the little islands to the south. And more importantly, we can explore each other.'

Her whole body was screaming at her to say yes. It was more tempting than she could put into words. But her brain was kicking and shouting, because a week on his yacht was just the kind of vulnerability that she'd learned to avoid like the plague. She would be completely at his whim, completely at his command. If she was wrong about him, and he wasn't trustworthy and decent, then what?

Only, she wasn't wrong.

She knew that.

In a way she'd never felt about Steven, she fundamentally understood Zeus, and knew that, just as he'd said, he'd never hurt her.

A week on his yacht. A week away from Athens. Away from his business. A week where she could pretend it was just him, and her, and all the reasons she had for meeting him in the first place didn't exist. A sneaky little cheat, a bubble, a break from agonising over what she should do. Because a week on his yacht had a definitive beginning, a middle and an end, and when that end came, he would drop her back in a port, she'd get to a plane and go home, away from him, and the most beautifully complicated, utterly addictive man and situation she'd ever known.

'I say yes,' she whispered, and then she smiled, because in the midst of her angsting a solution had come that just made sense. 'Yes, yes, yes.' And they both laughed as though neither had a care in the world.

* * *

Another first, he thought, as later that night his driver deposited them at the marina. Having been to her hotel, waiting for Jane to pack up her things, his patience was at an all-time low. He wanted to be alone with her, more than he could say.

It wasn't like they'd be completely alone on the yacht—there was a full-time captain, a cook and a housekeeper, but it was more than big enough for the staff to have their own quarters, leaving Zeus and Jane free to explore one another, just as he'd promised.

Promised on a whim. Without any forethought or planning. Promised because she'd thrown a date at him that seemed too soon for how much he enjoyed her company. And yet, he'd felt relief, most of all. Because she was going, and when Jane left, everything in his life would be so much simpler. Without her here to crave, he would simply move on, refocus on Philomena, or someone like her. A sensible, easy-going wife who would be just as pragmatic about the union as he'd be, who would never threaten his independence or equilibrium. At some point, the matter of children would become an issue, but that was also a pragmatic decision, and he intended to foreshadow it with whomever he married.

Until then, he had a week with Jane, and he intended to enjoy every damned minute of that week, until she was out of his system once and for all. It wasn't normal to obsess over someone like this. It sure as hell wasn't normal for Zeus. But he wasn't worried. A week gave them time, and at the end of it, no matter what, he'd let her go and focus on the thing that mattered most to him in the world: securing his future as sole owner of the Papandreo Group. Jane was just a blip in his life, and after this week, he'd remember that.

It probably wasn't even really about Jane. At least, not completely. Three months ago, his mother had died. After more than a decade of preparing for it, of knowing it was coming, it had still fractured parts of him he hadn't realised could be touched any longer. Then, two weeks ago, his father had told him about his affair, about the daughter he'd fathered and financially supported all her life. And there'd been such longing in Aristotle's face, such regret, that Zeus had known that the older man wasn't going to let it go, either. As far as he was concerned, that was his daughter, as much as Zeus was his son. A muscle jerked in his jaw as angry defiance surged through him.

All the touchstones of his life were shaking—as if a large earthquake were persistently rumbling the foundations of his existence. And then there was Jane. A light in the dark. A distraction from everything. A reprieve.

After this week, he'd have to face reality. He'd have to get serious about shoring up his position in the company. He'd have to marry. For the first time, contemplating that brought an acrid taste to his mouth and he ground his teeth, wishing he could rebel against the provision of the company's founding documents.

Except…

Were it not for that provision, Aristotle's love child would have an even greater claim on all things Papandreo, wouldn't she? At least the provision gave a black-

and-white requirement of ownership. He tried not to imagine her. He knew nothing about her yet—he was still waiting on information from the detective he'd hired—but he supposed it would not be difficult for anyone to propose a marriage like the one he was intending on offering to Philomena. Autonomy, independence, freedom, unimaginable wealth and, one day, a child, when the time was right. What if she'd already found someone willing to undertake marriage on those terms?

A bead of perspiration formed at the nape of his neck, but he refused to give in to that now.

He was here, with Jane, and he was going to damn well enjoy the week. After that, he'd put everything in motion for the rest of his life. A life without Jane in it.

'Let me guess,' she murmured, looking at the boats in the marina, a fingertip pressed to her perfectly shaped lips, so the unpleasantness of his thoughts evaporated on a sharp wave of need. 'Yours is—' she scanned the line of craft '—that one.'

She pointed to a reasonably sized boat with a gleaming 'P' on the side. 'No, that's the Petrakises'.'

'Oh.' She frowned, went back to looking and then her eyes widened when they landed on a boat so much larger than the others that it almost didn't register at first. 'Not that one?'

He saw the amazement on her features and laughed. 'You'd prefer to bob around at sea in one of these?' He gestured to the small boats in front of them.

'I'm not complaining.' She winked, all beautifully confident and charming, so his gut twisted sharply as his cells seemed to tighten.

'I'm glad. I'd hate to disappoint you.'

'That seems unlikely.'

He grinned, reaching down and taking her hand. 'Shall we?'

Of course, the yacht wasn't just enormous, but also incredibly luxuriously appointed, from the gleaming white accents to the shining timber features, and walls of glass that showed the ocean to best advantage. The moon bounced off the marina and the other boats as the captain readied the Papandreo yacht for departure, and Zeus left Jane alone a moment to speak with his crew. The driver of his car had unpacked her bags—Zeus, she presumed, had his own things on board already, for he brought nothing. And then, while Zeus was still absent, the yacht began to move, pushing back carefully from the pontoon and drifting into the clear water behind the rows of yachts, executing a perfect manoeuvre that enabled them to be pointing towards the Saronic Gulf.

Overhead, stars glittered brightly against a sky that was all black velvet, and Jane sighed a happy, contented sigh as the boat seemed to glide atop the water with effortless ease.

She was so focused on the boat's journey that she didn't notice Zeus's approach. It was only when he came to stand behind her and slid his hands around her waist, eased her hair over one shoulder so he could press his lips to the sensitive flesh in the curve of her neck, and she shivered. Not from cold, but from a total bodily awareness of him. A need that was in overdrive. It was as though being here, on the open water, somehow freed her from all restraint. Not just of the conundrum of her deception, but of the hurts of her past. Finally, for the first time in years, she felt almost liberated from the shadow of what Steven had done to her, of how he'd made her feel.

She felt, simply, free.

She turned slowly, smiling, unaware of the way the silver light of the moon caught her face and made it shimmer, the way her eyes sparkled, and her hair seemed to glow. 'Tell me something,' she prompted, linking her hands behind his back.

'Anything.'

Her heart trembled with a rush of power. 'Anything? Hmm. Perhaps I'll change my question, then.'

His gaze roamed her face in a way that pulled at her stomach. 'What would you like to know, *agapiméni*?'

'Your name,' she said. 'It's kind of unique.'

He grinned. 'You don't think it suits me?'

'On the contrary, there is something kind of godlike about you,' she murmured, then laughed at his raised brows. 'You have this kind of…all-powerful vibe going on.'

'Do I?'

She nodded.

'In what way?'

'Fishing for compliments?'

'Curious as to how you see me.'

'Well, like the fact you're happy to let me call the shots with what happens between us, erm, physically.' She glanced over his shoulder, cheeks flushing with warmth. 'I think a lot of guys would have egos that were too fragile for that.'

'Maybe you haven't been involved with the right kind of men before,' he said gently, though, so her heart trembled. The boat glided out of the marina fully and into the bay. She leaned back against the railing, eyes hooked to Zeus's face.

'Well, that's definitely true.'

'Including the man who hurt you?' he prompted, his tone light, but she felt the push of his enquiry, his desire to know and understand her.

'Definitely him,' she murmured.

'And since him?'

She shook her head a little. 'No one serious.'

His eyes bore into hers like beams. 'Why not?'

She stilled. The feeling of freedom wavered a little. Her throat tightened. She blinked away from Zeus, but he squeezed her waist. 'He can't hurt you anymore.'

She shook her head. 'It's not that.'

'You don't want to talk about it?'

She shook her head. 'I don't want to think about him,' she said, pulling a face. 'He's ruined enough of my life. I'm not going to let him ruin this, too.'

'Jane...' His hand moved over her hip gently. 'What did he do to you?'

She opened her mouth to tell him she *really* wanted to talk about something else, but then her eyes found his and something strange happened. Something powerful and altering. She looked at him and felt that bubble of freedom again, or rather, a bridge to freedom.

Maybe talking about it would help? Maybe talking

about it was what she needed? Lottie was the only person she'd spoken to about it in the past, and even then she'd found it hard to give more than a cursory explanation as to what had happened. She'd lived with a sense of all-consuming shame and grief, rather than admit how awful it had all been.

'We were dating,' she said with a rise of her shoulders. A breeze lifted off the ocean, so her hair shifted around her face, and she smelled the salt of the sea and the sweetness of her conditioner. Zeus caught the blond hairs and tamed them behind one of her ears, his hand remaining at her shoulder. Warm, silently encouraging her to continue. 'I met him through a mutual friend, and I liked him straight away. I was seventeen, he was older, so naturally, I thought he was way, way cooler than me,' she said with a hint of self-deprecating humour, even though it wasn't remotely funny. 'A lot of my friends had started seeing guys, hooking up at parties. I kind of felt weird that I wasn't into hooking up or whatever.'

'You were only seventeen,' he pointed out.

She pulled a face. 'I somehow suspect you'd already notched up some experience by that age.'

His jaw tightened a little. 'Not as much as you'd think.'

'Really?'

'My mother wasn't well. It took a lot of my focus.'

'Oh, gosh. I'm sorry.'

He nodded once, dismissively. She felt his pain, though, and moved a little closer to him. He was so warm, so strong, being this close did something to her insides. Somehow, just his proximity flooded her with those qualities, too—warmth and strength—as though they were completely contagious.

'Anyway,' she continued. 'I met him and liked him. He was funny and handsome, smart, and I guess he gave me the one thing I'd been missing.'

Zeus waited quietly.

'Attention. He made me feel as though I was the centre of his world.' She shook her head with frustration at how stupid and trusting she'd been. 'I took everything at face value. I really thought he loved me.'

'He didn't?'

She shook her head. 'I doubt it.'

'Why?'

'After...that night,' she said on a soft exhalation, 'he was so...'

'What happened that night?' Zeus asked, and now his voice had a gruff urgency to it that pulled at her and made her whole body seem as though it were flying.

'It was another party. We'd all been drinking. A lot. And I didn't really drink much at all, so you can imagine how a few glasses of champagne would have gone to my head, let alone the bottle or so I had. He kept bringing me drinks,' she muttered, back in time now, in that awful night. But somehow, the sting of it had faded, and talking to Zeus seemed to be taking away the last vestiges of power of that night to wound her. She marvelled at that, revelled in the sensation of freedom, even as she continued speaking. 'I'd told him I wasn't ready for—sex. I wasn't. I liked him. I thought I even loved him, but I didn't want to just have sex with him. I wasn't ready,' she repeated, as though Zeus understanding that was fundamentally important.

'Which was always your decision and right,' he said. Like he had a hotwire into her brain and knew *just* what to say.

'I started to feel a little sick. So much champagne,' she muttered. 'He said he'd find somewhere quiet for me to lie down.'

Zeus swore, darkness crossing his handsome features. 'Go on.' But the words were muted, as if uttered through gritted teeth, and she realised that this was hurting him, more than it was her.

'I'm okay, Zeus. It was a long time ago,' she assured him, softly.

'Go on,' he repeated as if he had braced himself for the rest and now needed to hear it.

She expelled a shaking breath. 'I don't remember a lot of it. The room was dark,' she said, voice trembling. 'His hands were rough.' She swallowed past a lump in her throat. 'I told him "no." I'm sure of it, though he disagreed the next day.'

Zeus nodded once, his lips held so tightly they were white rimmed. But his touch was gentle, his eyes sympathetic.

'I didn't want it to happen. I know that much. He was heavy on top of me. He smelt of beer and sweat. And it hurt. I think I passed out. I don't know.' And even though she felt somehow liberated from the memory, tears sparkled on her lashes now. She blinked away. 'So that was my first—and only—time.'

He was quiet and still for what seemed an age. The

hum of the boat formed a background noise; the splashing of the waves against the sides of the craft occasionally flicked them with tiny droplets of salted water, but really, it was just the two of them, in the sort of bubble that was formed by the sharing of one's deepest secrets.

Then Zeus lifted his hands to her cheeks, cupped her face gently, holding her steady, his own body so powerful and large but not at all scary or intimidating. 'You were raped, Jane,' he said, stroking her cheek with his thumb. 'You were raped by someone you cared for, someone you trusted. It's the most natural thing in the world that you have carried that wound with you all these years.'

She opened her mouth to dispute what he'd said. *Rape* sounded so jarring, so violent, but of course, that was exactly what had happened to her. She hadn't consented to sleeping with Steven; she hadn't even been *able* to consent, given how drunk she'd been. He took what he wanted, regardless of how that impacted her.

A tear slid down her cheek. Not a tear of sadness, but rather relief, because she felt not only seen by Zeus, but also accepted. Understood. Valued.

'Have you spoken to someone?'

'Other than you?' she asked, the attempt at humour falling flat. Neither of them was in a humorous mood.

'A therapist. Someone qualified to help you.'

'No,' she whispered. 'It took me a long time to accept what had happened. Longer still to tell anyone—my best friend—about that night. I just couldn't… I felt…'

He waited, patiently.

'I blamed myself,' she whispered, shaking her head, squeezing her eyes shut.

'But you know now that you weren't to blame.' He said it as a statement, but she knew he was asking her.

She bit into her lower lip. 'I know that if the same thing had happened to my best friend, I would say exactly that to her. It's not your fault. It's just hard to look back on that night without regret. Why did I drink so much? Why did I go into a room with him? Why didn't I fight harder?'

'You shouldn't have had to fight. You trusted him. You loved him. He took advantage of your youth, your love, your inexperience, your drunkenness, your trust. It was a brutal betrayal. By every metric, this was his fault, not yours.'

She knew that. Of course she did. But understanding something academically didn't always equate to how one felt. She nodded slowly, anyway, because she couldn't fault his logic.

'I presume you didn't press charges?'

She shook her head. 'I wish I had, if only to stop him from doing the same thing to someone else,' she muttered. 'But it took me too long to process it all myself, let alone going to the police. And when I confronted him about it when we broke up, he made it clear that he would tell anyone a very different version of that night, paint me as someone who just regretted getting drunk and having sex, rather than what had actually happened.'

A muscle ticked in Zeus's jaw and the strength of his emotions seemed to barrage across at her.

'This man is not worthy of the title,' he spat after a

pause. 'Your body is *your* body,' he said slowly, enunciating each word in his deep, husky voice. 'Yours to pleasure, yours to control, yours in every way. No man has the right to touch you if you do not want that.'

She nodded, a lump forming in her throat. These were all things she knew, but again, hearing Zeus say them was like treacle running over dry wood. It soaked in, softened everything.

'Afterwards, I just couldn't be with a man without feeling…scared,' she admitted. 'I tried. I dated. But any time a man would kiss me, I'd freeze up. I couldn't bear it,' she confessed, eyes latching to his. 'And then, I met you…' Her voice trailed off, because she couldn't explain what it was about Zeus that had somehow overcome those barriers. 'And I just felt…safe,' she finished huskily, not meeting his eyes, because revealing that to him somehow made a part of her seem too vulnerable.

'You are safe,' he promised, dropping his hands to her waist and pulling her against him, brushing her lips with his own. 'I promised you that, and I meant it.'

'I know.' She smiled then, a weak smile, but one that was filled with all the light of her soul. 'It's not just that you make me feel safe, though,' she continued her confession.

'No?'

'Honestly, I thought any sexual side of me died that night with Steven. I thought he'd killed the parts of me that were responsible for getting turned on. But then I met you, and everything screamed back to life. It's like you flicked a switch inside me and I feel…'

His eyes flared when they met hers. 'If nothing else,'

he said, moving his hands to her back and bunching the fabric of her dress there, 'let me give you that, this week. Let me give you all the pleasure, all the knowledge, all the awakenings you have missed out on.'

She blinked up at him, something like awe building inside her. And more than that, she had the strangest sense of fate winding around them, as if each star was flicking a single piece of thread towards them, and as the boat cut through the dark waters of the gulf, those threads landed on Jane, and Zeus, and tangled together, wrapping them up, cocooning them in this place, this time, but somehow, also for all time. No matter what happened, this week would always be solely, completely, theirs, like an imprint of a moment that simply couldn't fade.

She nodded slowly, though it hadn't been a question so much as a pledge. She nodded because with all of her heart, with all of her soul, she agreed with him.

CHAPTER EIGHT

THE LAST THING Zeus felt like employing was restraint. From the moment he'd first seen Jane Fisher, he'd wanted her. He'd imagined her naked in his bed, utterly at his command. But even that night in the bar, he'd sensed a fragility to her. Despite her over-the-top beauty, her apparent confidence, something about her had urged him to be cautious. Careful. As though he might break her; as though she'd been broken before.

And she had been.

She'd been broken, and no one had helped put her back together again. She'd done that all herself, and even though she was strong and living her life, she wasn't fully embracing all of herself, nor all aspects of her life.

For that, she wanted him, and showing her what sex *should* be like would be one of the greatest privileges of his life.

So long as he could be true to his word and slow everything down. The last thing he wanted to do was overwhelm her with his own needs.

This wasn't about Zeus, but Jane.

He pulled her against his chest and kissed her. Slowly. Gently. His mouth probing hers. Tasting, teasing, tempting, until she was moaning against him, the softness of her body, the way her curves pressed to his chest, the warmth of her skin, her fragrance. It all hummed and buzzed and made him feel as though he were walking on a tightrope with a death-defying fall in both directions.

She said his name, a groan, a plea, a curse, and he felt it. He felt it deep in his soul; her tone matched his own.

Her hands pushed at his shirt, lifting it, her fingertips brushing his bare skin, pushing the shirt until it lifted higher, her palms flat against his hair-roughened chest, his nipples, so he bit back a curse in reflexive shock at how damned great that felt.

'Jane.' His voice held a warning, because he was not actually a god, and maintaining control when she touched him like that would take every ounce of his strength. But then he looked at her and realised: it didn't matter. It didn't matter how much it cost him; he would do this for her. She could touch. She could explore. She could feel. Be curious, taste, touch, and he would let her, even when he was holding on by a single thread, because she deserved that. Because he'd promised it to her.

So, he stood still as granite, as she pushed the shirt higher. 'Arms, please,' she murmured, eyes flicking to his with a mix of uncertainty and passion.

He lifted them, and she guided the shirt off his body completely, dropping it to the deck at their sides. More uncertainty in the depths of her gaze as she glanced at him and then leaned forward, pressing those perfectly shaped lips to his pec, flicking him with her tongue, expelling a long, shaky breath that covered him in warmth, before moving her mouth lower, towards his nipple. She rolled her tongue over it first, then her whole mouth, sucking there for a moment before moving to the other, and her hands drew invisible circles over his sides, her fingers light enough to raise his skin in goosebumps.

'You're beautiful,' she said after a moment, moving her kiss to his shoulder, nipping him with her teeth. 'Godlike,' she added, her smile teasing now.

He was only capable of making a grunting sound in response.

'May I?' She reached for his pants, but he shook his head once, aware that the closer he got to naked, the harder this was going to be.

'You first,' he suggested, but carefully, gently, in case he was rushing her.

Their eyes met, her cheeks flushed pink, and he tilted her chin with his finger, demanding her eyes hold his. 'If you want. Only ever if you want.'

She nodded once. 'I know that. You don't need to say it.'

'I do. I need to say it each and every time, so you understand…'

'You're not him,' she said, simply. 'I know you'd never do what he did. I trust you.'

Trust. She trusted him.

Zeus closed his eyes for a moment, because it was such a monumental gift. Zeus knew that more than anyone. He'd spent his entire adult life walking alongside a deep sense of mistrust. Not of people, but of life in general. Of getting close to anyone, because of the unreliability of the future. Trust was not something he gave easily, so he appreciated Jane offering it to him now, and in the back of his mind, he wondered if maybe she might just be the one person who could make him reciprocate that. To trust her.

He'd frozen, but Jane hadn't. Her hands were reaching for the hem of her skirt, lifting it up her body, revealing another pair of silky panties and this time, a matching bra, so he was sucked right back into the moment by the sight of her on the deck of his boat dressed in only underwear and heels, her blond hair whipping around her face in a magnificently sensual display of the elements.

And all the power of thought dissipated, leaving him to act purely on instincts. The instinct to pleasure, to worship, to protect, all bound up together, guiding each and every one of his actions.

He lifted her easily and carried her, cradled to his bare chest, across the deck to one of the large, square sun lounges. The mattress was soft, a pale grey, and he placed Jane down on it reverently, before standing to look at her, committing this sight to memory.

Because trust was overrated, and the one thing he knew for certain was that they had this one week together. After that, she would be gone from his life, and he was okay with that. Much safer to accept her time constraints than start wanting more. So long as he could always remember just how perfect she'd been.

He brought his body over hers, careful to support his weight on his knees and elbows, kissing her with all the softness he'd used before, gently, so that it was Jane who deepened the kiss, pushing up onto her elbows to claim more of him, to encourage him to take more of her, too. And so he did. He kissed her back with the same intensity, until they were both panting, and her hands were roaming his body frantically, their hands moving in unison to remove first her bra and then her panties, her desperate longing sending arrows of need shooting through every part of his body.

He moved his kiss to the curve of her neck, teasing her sensitive pulse point there, then lower, to worship her beautiful round breasts, first with his mouth, until she was whimpering and arching her back in an ancient, primal sign of need, then his hands, which cupped their fullness, teased her taut nipples, while his mouth moved lower to the apex of her thighs. She screamed his name as her whole body tightened with the approach of her orgasm and he grinned against her, but didn't stop, because hot on the heels of his name came her plea for more. More, more, over and over, and her hands pushed through his hair, tussling in its length, as if that could save her from the inevitable tumble. Then, with a push of her feet into the soft mattress, she was lifting her pelvis, a guttural cry spilling from her lips as her whole body was racked by the release of her pleasure.

'Zeus,' she groaned moments later, while her breath was still coming in fits. 'That's... I... You're...'

He propped his chin on her abdomen, eyes holding hers with a mixture of need and amusement. 'Lost for words, Jane?'

She flicked his shoulder and collapsed back against the mattress. 'You know you definitely live up to your name in this department, right?' she demanded, pushing up onto her elbows so she could see him better.

'All positive feedback gratefully received.'

She laughed softly, but then she was quiet, and he felt the mood shift inside her.

'What is it?'

'I want to see you,' she said, simply. 'I haven't even... You're always dressed.'

'Ah,' he said with a mock-sombre nod. 'With good reason. I'm a ticking time bomb, and you, *agapaméni*, hold the fuse.'

'Why can't we light it?'

'Because we're not ready.'

'We're not?'

He shook his head, pushing up her body.

'I feel ready,' she disputed.

He hesitated, because wasn't that sort of the point? That this was up to Jane, to call the shots? He didn't want to disregard her wishes, but he needed to be sure. She'd said she trusted him; he wasn't going to abuse that trust.

'And you'll still feel ready tomorrow,' he promised. He kissed her lips and pulled her against his side, her naked body so utterly perfect and tempting that he honestly thought he deserved some kind of medal for holding back. Again.

'Tell me a story,' she murmured, head resting on his chest.

He thought about that for a moment. 'What would you like to hear?'

'Tell me about you,' she said. 'Tell me what it was like growing up as Zeus Papandreo.' She stifled a yawn as he began to slowly stroke her back, drawing lines along the edge of her spine.

'One of my earliest memories,' he began, 'was out on the water.'

Another yawn.

'My *yaya* was from an old fishing village, and when she married my grandfather, she stepped into a world of unimaginable wealth and comfort. Though theirs was, I have to say, a very traditional arranged marriage.'

'Arranged?' She shifted slightly so she could look up at him.

He made a noise of agreement. 'Our family business is bound up in a conservative clause that requires whoever is at the helm to have married before taking ownership. It's been that way for hundreds of years.'

Jane's skin paled slightly and he half laughed.

'Don't worry, Jane. I'm not building up to a proposal.'

She glanced away quickly, her eyes impossible to read when they were focused anywhere but him.

'I didn't mean—'

'Nor did I,' he assured her. 'Anyway, my grandfather proposed when he was twenty years old, and my *yaya* was only eighteen,' he said with a shake of his head. 'She went from living a modest life in a salty old village to suddenly being at the front and centre of Greek's elite.'

'That must have been a huge adjustment,' Jane murmured, though there was something in her voice that still spoke of hesitation.

'She took it in her stride, apparently,' Zeus said. 'But she never forgot her roots, and my grandfather didn't want her to. They came out onto the bay often. Not in a boat like this—*yaya* would turn over in her grave,' he admitted with a throaty laugh. 'This is not her idea of a boat. For her, you had to be able to feel the movements, touch the sea, to know that the ocean is a living beast, requiring respect and fear, awe.'

Jane sighed. 'That sounds so romantic.'

'It might sound romantic. In reality, I spent a lot of the time that first year hanging over the edge, losing my lunch to seasickness.'

She laughed at that. 'Less romantic.'

'A lot less.' He flashed her a grin. 'But she was determined to turn me into a fisherman, of sorts.'

'What about your father?'

'It was never his thing.'

'And you?'

'I loved it. After I got over the shock of the open waters in a boat not much bigger than a car,' he laughed. 'I swear she did it just to throw me in at the deep end. But it worked. There was something so thrilling about being out there with them, feeling the turn and churn of the waves, knowing that I had to keep my wits about me and rely on the people I was with.' His voice took on a slightly harder edge then, because he'd often reflected on how false the message had been that his grandparents had taught him.

To rely on your shipmates, and everything would be fine.

Even when it simply wasn't possible to give such a guarantee in this life.

Zeus's expression tightened but he quickly dispelled the thought, because Jane's breathing was growing slow and rhythmic, her head heavy against his chest. He reached down beside him to a basket that held several rolled-up blankets and unfurled one over her. Anything to keep her just like this.

'What else?' she murmured groggily, so he resumed the gentle rubbing of her back, even as her eyes drifted shut.

He began to speak then of the time their boat had almost capsized, but he kept his voice soft and low, and after a few minutes she was fast asleep, and he was glad. He rested his head back into the pillows and tried not to think about his childhood anymore. Not about those halcyon days, when the sun had shone, and the water had been cool and reassuring and everything had seemed impossibly perfect. Not about the way his mother's diagnosis had dislodged every bit of his certainty and overpowered him with anger and doubt. Not about the way her death had changed him, permanently. He tried to focus purely on the here and now, on how good Jane felt pressed to his side, and as he drifted off to sleep, whilst his brain was occupying that liminal space between waking and not, he let himself imagine that she was the woman he proposed to, after all, and that rather than a cold, practical marriage of convenience, he ended up with someone warm and perfect, in all the ways he'd long ago learned to mistrust…

The lightest breeze rustled her hair, brushing it over her shoulders and face, making her reach up and scratch her nose, and then, when her hand fell back down, it connected with a warm, bare chest, and her eyes flared open in confusion for a moment. She was disoriented. One part of her was in her flat in London, one part in the hotel in Athens. Then she remembered, and she blinked her eyes around them, smiling a little to realise they'd fallen asleep on the deck of the boat. It had continued to travel through the night; the mainland was now in the far, far distance. She sighed; the sense of freedom she'd begun to enjoy the night before exploding through her in waves now.

It was barely morning. The sky was a hue of pale silver with touches of peach and orange, and the water had a steely grey colour. The moon was still overhead, shimmering like a splotch of white paint. She angled her face, studying Zeus still asleep, and something in her chest twisted hard and plummeted all the way down to her toes.

She didn't want to think about the future. She didn't want to think about Lottie, about the marriage clause in the family business's contracts; she didn't want to think about anything outside of this bubble. Maybe it was naive of her, but she needed to believe they could enjoy this week without any of those complications having an impact.

And more than that, she simply needed him.

Her cheeks flushed as she remembered her dreams and how they'd been flooded by wild, and very *not* PG images of Zeus. Partly memories, partly fantasies. She moved her finger over his chest, idly drawing circles around his nipples, before she smiled again, this time a smile of pure impishness, and moved her naked body over him, straddling him, before quickly leaning down and kissing his lips. He moaned, his hands instinctively coming to rest at her hips, his fingers pressing into the top of her bottom, so she dropped her waist, her sex connecting with his still-clothed erection, and she smiled against his mouth at the proof of how much he wanted this. Despite his patience. Maybe because of it?

'Jane,' he said, eyes bursting open and landing on hers.

'You said I'd still be ready today, and you were right.' She dragged his lower lip between her teeth, then deepened their kiss. 'I'm so, so ready, Zeus.'

His hands began to stroke her naked back, her bottom, her thighs, touching her all over, both gentle and demanding, the perfect combination; she pressed herself hard against his arousal, finding her sensitive cluster of nerves and shamelessly using him to stimulate that pleasure centre until it was almost impossible to breathe, and her eyes were filled with stars. His hands brushed over her breasts, and she cried out, because every part of her was so overly sensitive. It was like she was a forest of dry wood, and he'd struck a match, so bit by bit, she was burning up, and all she could do was admire the ferocity of the fire.

'Please,' she said, simply. 'I want you.'

He stilled, staring up into her face and then, to Jane's relief, he nodded once, kissing her as he began to remove his trousers, kicking them off before reaching for them as an afterthought and removing a condom from one of the pockets.

'You came prepared,' she said with relief.

'Naturally.'

Her cheeks flushed pink, because she hadn't even thought of that.

He placed the condom on the edge of the mattress and went back to kissing her, but with Jane on top, she felt so powerful, so in control of where she was touching him, of how fast they were going, and that control was addictive. His trousers were removed, but his boxers were still in place, and suddenly, she wanted, more than anything, to see *him*. To touch him. Her hands caught at the waistband of his shorts, and she began to push them down, but he stilled her to say, 'Jane, I should warn you—'

She glanced up at him.

'I'm big.'

Her brows shot up.

'I promise I won't hurt you.'

Curiosity now had her moving faster, pulling his shorts down just low enough to see that he was not exaggerating, even a little bit. He was huge. Long, wide and rock, rock-hard.

Her jaw dropped.

'I—see what you mean.'

'We'll take it slow,' he promised.

She couldn't look away from him.

'If you keep staring at me like that, Jane, this really isn't going to last very long.'

Reluctantly, her gaze travelled the length of his body.

'I'm— To be fair, I haven't seen a man's body in a very long time—'

His expression darkened then, and she knew why. Neither of them wanted to contemplate Steven in the context of this. He moved then, catching her and flipping her onto her back, bringing his body over hers.

'Remember, *agapaméni*, you are in charge. Always.'

She nodded, her heart soaring towards her throat as he unfurled the condom over his length. But rather than separating her thighs and taking her, instead, he returned to kissing her, then her breasts, then her sex, until she was incandescent once more and so wet for him, she could feel it between her legs. 'God, Zeus,' she cried out, and only then did he nudge her legs apart and press himself to her sex, holding there a moment as he wrapped her into a hug and pressed her to his chest, whispering Greek words in her ear. She stared above them at the dawn sky, painted the kind of palette she would never forget, even if it weren't the backdrop to such a moment, and slowly, gently, he pressed into her.

It had been so long for Jane, and she'd built it up to be such a terrifying event, she'd been so worried she might never have sex with anyone ever again. But in the end, in Zeus's arms, it neither hurt nor terrified her. It simply felt…perfect.

He *was* big, and at first, she experienced discomfort to accommodate him, but only at first. He gave her space to get used to his strength and size before he began to move, and all the while, he alternated between whispering in her ear in his native language and kissing her throat, her lips, her earlobe; and his hands—those awesome, talented hands—roamed her body, enslaving her breasts before one moved to her sex and began to brush over her there, in the same tempo as his movements, so whatever his arousal had been stirring within her, it was no longer possible to take it slowly. She was tumbling headfirst into a star-filled abyss, flooded with light and sparkle, magic and warmth, and she revelled in the cataclysmic explosion, with the fading stars above, the pale moon, the peachy-pink sky the witness to the most sublimely blissful event in Jane Fisher's entire twenty-four years.

CHAPTER NINE

THE FIRST PORT the boat stopped in was on Crete, at the ancient city of Heraklion, which they explored on foot. Jane was in awe of the history, transfixed by the beauty and so captivated that she hardly had time to think about what had happened that morning. When she *did* think about it, her cheeks flushed and her lips twisted into a smile, because it had been perfect. Not just what had happened between them on the deck, but afterwards, too. When he'd walked with her, hand in hand, into the yacht to a palatial bathroom, so she could shower. He'd offered her space, but she'd shaken her head because she didn't *want* space. She'd wanted him. More touching. More feeling. More kissing.

He'd stirred something to life inside her and it was turning out to be quite insatiable.

They'd showered together, loofah-ing one another with sudsy bubbles, kissing, laughing, worshipping some more, and when they were finished, he wrapped her in a towel and gave her a brief tour of a small section of the boat—ending in his bedroom. They'd stayed there, in bed, until the boat had stopped moving and

Zeus had glanced through the windows and commented, 'We're in port. Fancy some exploring?'

She'd been reluctant to leave the boat, which had been obvious to Zeus. He laughed. 'Just for a few hours, *agapaméni*. We'll be back soon.'

In the end, she was glad she'd agreed, because Heraklion was incredible. Not just beautiful, though it was that; the city was charged with a strange energy. As though all the layers of its history were still here, somehow, caught between the wide streets and stone buildings.

'Hungry?'

She hadn't realised it until now, but she was famished. 'Definitely.'

'I know a place.' He gestured with his hand, then caught hers in his, and glanced down at her. Jane's eyes met his and she almost lost her footing, so powerful was the sense of something flashing between them. She smiled quickly and out of nowhere, thought of Lottie and her duty to her best friend, and her whole body seemed to weaken.

'Here.' He gestured again to a charming little restaurant. The glass-panelled door was painted a bright blue, the awnings above the windows were blue-and-white-striped and the chairs on the sidewalk were white wrought iron. At each table, there was a small vase with a single carnation placed inside. It was quaint and charming, rustic and old-fashioned, everything Jane adored, but she felt slightly off-kilter in that moment, with the mental reminder of how duplicitous this all was.

Except it wasn't, she reminded herself forcibly. She

was here with Zeus for one week. That was all. It didn't matter that she'd been sent by Lottie with a ploy to delay his ability to propose to anyone else. It didn't matter that meeting him hadn't been fate or an accident, but rather part of Lottie's scheme. It didn't even matter that if she ever had to make a choice between Lottie and Zeus, she would choose Lottie—of course she would, because they had been best friends for over a decade, and each woman meant the world to the other. She'd never have to make that choice, though, because Zeus would never know about Jane's connection to Lottie. This week was safe from all of that.

She exhaled as they were shown to a table by the window, and Jane was glad to be sitting inside, in the air-conditioning, rather than at the tables on the sidewalk. As charming as they were, the afternoon sun was beating down and she suspected it would be unbearably hot to sit there and eat.

They ordered calamari and a salad and a glass each of white wine, and while they ate, Zeus mostly talked about the island. Lottie had a very soft recollection of its history, courtesy of school classes, but nothing had really sunk in. Zeus, she discovered, was somewhat of an expert.

'How do you know all this?' Jane asked as coffee was delivered, along with a single enormous slice of *ketaifi*.

Zeus seemed to hesitate. 'My mother loved history. When she was unwell, I would read her books—histories, historical accounts, myths. She loved it all. She was incredibly proud to be Greek,' he said, one side of his lips twisting in what might have been described as a smile by someone who'd never seen his *actual* smile. Something heavy thudded in her stomach. Guilt.

Because Zeus's mother had died only recently, and yet he was carrying on as though everything was fine and normal. But surely, he was still grieving her?

'You said she was sick?'

His lips tightened, outlined by white. 'Yes.'

Which was shorthand for, 'can we not talk about it'?

But if they were to know one another only for the rest of this week, then Jane wanted to *really* know him. To leave no stone unturned. It wasn't as though she'd be able to pick up the phone in a month's time and ask him whatever she'd forgotten to ask now. Leaving Zeus would be a one-way trip.

'And you helped care for her?'

He flinched slightly, looked towards the window. Walling himself off from her. Beneath the table, she pushed one foot forward so she could stroke his ankle.

'We had nurses,' he answered, reluctantly. Slowly. 'Around-the-clock care, in the end.'

Jane nodded, but he wasn't looking at her.

'My father preferred to stay by her side. I took over the business at her lowest points, when he couldn't bear to leave.'

He painted a bleak picture, though he spoke of it with such sparing words. 'It went on for a while?'

Zeus turned to face her then, held her gaze for several beats before reaching for his coffee—thick and dark. Again, she thought of Lottie with a pang in her chest.

'Her first diagnosis was when I was nine years old.'

Jane closed her eyes against the pain of that.

'It became normal,' he said, stiffly. Coldly. In a way that was rehearsed. Like he'd said this before, or at least thought it. 'She was sick, and then she wasn't. Periods of remission were, at first, like the sun, breaking through after a fierce storm. The sheer sense of relief was almost crippling. But then she became sick again. Then better, then sick. I stopped expecting recovery—or even for her periods of wellness to last. Every day she felt good was a gift, but I knew, I always knew, it was temporary.'

Jane shook her head, trying to stem the tears that were making her eyes sting. She didn't know what to say. She personally knew people who *had* recovered from cancer. Who'd gone into remission and stayed there. What Zeus's mother had experienced sounded like an unbearably aggressive and harrowing form of the disease.

'I'm so sorry,' was all she could say, the words slightly tremulous.

'It's life,' he said, and for all that her voice had been rich with emotion, his was utterly devoid of it. Even his eyes were cold when they met hers. Cold in a way she'd never expected to see in Zeus. Ruthlessly blanked of feeling, of sentiment. 'It's unpredictable and cruel.'

'Not always.'

'No?'

She shook her head. 'Most of the time, life is wonderful. And the unpredictable is part of what makes it so.'

He stared at her for several beats and then glanced back towards the window. 'We'll have to agree to disagree, *agapaméni*.'

But she didn't want that. She didn't want him to be

so burdened by his pain, by the unpredictability of his mother's illness, by the impact that had clearly had on him. They had one week together, and she couldn't bear to think of him living with such a dim view of the world.

'How is your father?' she asked, to draw his attention back to her and, obliquely, their conversation.

Zeus continued to stare out at the street, one of his large hands holding the small coffee cup in a way that, in other circumstances, she would have found amusing.

'In reference to my mother's death?'

'Yes.'

'It's complicated.'

Jane frowned. 'Why?'

Zeus turned to face her then, scanning her features as though he'd forgotten who she was, and Jane's heart went cold. After what they'd shared that morning, she didn't *ever* want him to look at her like that. She blinked away, tears stinging her eyes for another reason now.

'He loved her very much,' Zeus said, finally. 'They married young, essentially grew up together in many ways. She was his partner in every way. He is...bereft.'

Jane glanced back at him in time to catch an expression on his features that spoke of resentment. Anger. She frowned a little. There was more here than Zeus was telling her.

'And you?' she pushed, aware that he didn't want to be having this conversation but continuing regardless. 'You must also be bereft?'

'I was prepared for it.'

She flinched. 'Does that make a difference in the end?'

'It must.'

She shook her head, frustrated. Because he was stonewalling her. He was hiding his feelings rather than admit them. She *knew* Zeus now. She knew his emotions ran deep, and that he must still be feeling an enormous black hole of grief for the mother he'd only recently lost. Or was he so determined to conquer grief, to be strong over it, that he refused to accept it, even to himself?

'I knew it was coming, Jane. From when I was just a teenager, I had prepared myself for it. As I said, every day she was well was a gift, when she wasn't, it was… my baseline. I braced for her death, and in the end, she was in so much pain, barely lucid. It was a release for her. I know it was.'

A tear slid down Jane's cheek. He spoke so calmly, so sensibly, but Jane couldn't hear his description without feeling all the pain of what he was describing.

'Don't cry, please,' he insisted, reaching for a napkin so he could lean over the table and wipe her cheek gently.

'It's just… I'm so sad for you.'

'Don't be. Do I look sad?'

She looked at him and shook her head, but not to disagree, rather out of confusion. She couldn't fathom his feelings, and it bothered her. It was like he'd hardened his heart intentionally, because he knew that without taking that precaution, her death would hurt too, too much. She supposed it made a sort of sense. To pre-emptively cope with a wound that might otherwise have the power to cut you off at the knees. So, he'd emotionally withdrawn from the situation, while still supporting his father and mother.

But had he pulled all of his emotions back? Did that explain his string of short-term affairs and no serious girlfriends?

'Shall we get moving?' His voice was light, as though that conversation hadn't just taken place. Her eyes held his as her mind continued to ruminate, but she nodded.

'Sure, let's go.'

She knew, though, that no matter where they went, she wouldn't let the conversation drop completely. She'd started to see more of Zeus, had begun to understand him, and she wouldn't rest until that was complete. She had one week—she intended to use it fully.

The sunset was particularly beautiful, observed from the deck of the boat, which was moored in a cove on the other side of Crete, in the Gulf of Mesara. But it was not the most spectacular thing in Zeus's vision. No. That would be Jane, swimming in the crystal-clear waters just off the boat, as though she'd recently discovered she was, in fact, half mermaid.

She ducked and dived beneath the surface, spun pirouettes, then emerged for air, her big blue eyes surrounded by dark lashes courtesy of the water, her hair plastered to her head.

He'd heard the expression *breathtaking* without really understanding that it could describe an actual physical phenomenon. Right now, looking at her, it felt as though his breath had been squeezed from his lungs. And not in the way he'd felt when his mother had died. That had winded him, had made him feel as though his own body was losing life.

He'd braced for it, yes. Or thought he had. But how could one really brace for that sort of loss? Months later, he still found it almost impossible to believe he was living in a world that was absent his mother. In a way, her having been sick for as long as she was had made that a new kind of normal. He was used to going to his parents' place and taking up a book from the shelves, taking it to her and picking up wherever they'd left off. Or sometimes, she'd have something particular she wanted to hear about, and then she'd make a request of him, which he was always happy to oblige.

It had been three months, but the sense of being winded hadn't really eased.

His father's revelation about his affair and love child had been proverbial salt in the wound. It had hurt like the devil. To imagine his father sleeping with some other woman, while his mother suffered. While his mother faced what must have been every parent's worst nightmare: the idea of leaving behind a beloved small child.

'You're sure you don't want to swim?' she called up to him.

He'd initially demurred. He rarely swam in the ocean, though he couldn't really remember why. An old fear? A habit? A disinterest? There was a pool and spa on board. If he felt like swimming, he could use either of those.

But Jane's delight in the raw, elemental ocean was like a lightning bolt bursting through him. She looked so free and unburdened, and suddenly, an urge to dive into the ocean and let it wash away his grief—a grief he kept so firmly locked inside that no one, not even Jane, not even here, could know.

Before she could ask again, he was pushing out of his slides at the same time as removing his shirt.

Her delighted expression was the hammer in the nail of his decision. What wouldn't he give to see her features shine like that?

He took the steps down to the pontoon at the rear of the yacht, strode to the edge then dived in, surfacing right beside her. She spun to him and laughed, treading water easily, as though she swam often.

'You're like some kind of mermaid,' he observed, kissing her softly, because he couldn't resist.

'I like the water. Always have.'

He caught her around the waist and held her close, his legs taking over the work of keeping them afloat. 'Do you swim often?'

'I was on the team at school,' she replied. 'It was a lot of early starts.'

'And now?'

'Now I prefer to swim for pleasure. There's a Lido not far from my place. I go there a few times a week.' She looked around, her expression serene. 'It doesn't really compare to this, though.'

'No?'

She shook her head. 'You must love coming out here.'

He considered her, felt something churn in his chest. Her vivacity and love of life were just so palpable. Even after the betrayal she'd endured, the hurt she'd lived with, Jane had still managed to hold on to something rare and precious: positivity.

'Yes,' he agreed, simply, because she was right. He did love being on the water. It made him feel elemental and powerful again, but also human, because it was a stark reminder of how much more powerful the ocean was. 'Though I tend to swim on the boat.'

Her brows lifted skyward. 'There's a pool on the boat?'

He laughed. 'And a spa.'

She let out a low whistle. 'I mean, it's obviously fancy. I just didn't expect...' She trailed off and shrugged. 'I get the impression you work a lot,' she said after a beat. 'Does that leave much time for this?' She gestured towards the boat and then the sunset.

His eyes roamed her face, and he was transfixed. Not just by her beauty, but by the ability she had to ask the kinds of questions he usually sidestepped with ease, in just such a way that made him want to bare his soul to her.

It had to be because she was leaving within a week. There was a security that came from that, a certainty that no matter what happened between them, it wouldn't change either of their futures. He was destined for a pragmatic, sensible marriage, to jump through the hoops so he could inherit the company he'd always considered his by right. And she... He frowned reflexively. What did Jane's future hold?

She'd come into his life as a woman still carrying the wounds of her past, and in many ways, those wounds had broken her. But she was stirring back to life, becoming whole again; he could see that happening before his eyes. So, what did that mean? That she'd go home and instead of being repulsed when another man kissed her, might she lean into it? Start to enjoy the promise of flirtation and the spectre of sex?

He pulled away from her quickly, so she said his name on a short breath of surprise. 'What is it?'

'Nothing,' he lied. 'Let's swim.' He smiled, but it felt like a facsimile of the real deal, and he knew she saw that, because her face showed concern. He ignored it. He didn't want her concern, and he didn't want to contemplate what came next. Suddenly, the idea of Jane moving on from him sat like a rock in his gut.

They raced around the yacht until Jane's arms were like jelly and her legs were sore, as the sun slipped lower and lower towards the horizon, and then, as they passed the pontoon on the back, she stopped swimming and grabbed hold of the rails.

'I think I'm done,' she said, trying to keep her tone light, when there was something dark stirring inside her. A frustration, with the way he shut her down whenever she took the conversation in a direction he didn't want to go.

It *hurt*.

It hurt, after she'd told him about Steven. It hurt, because she'd trusted him.

But at the same time, it wasn't as though she didn't have secrets of her own. Like Lottie.

They didn't have to tell each other *everything*. Except, her friendship with Lottie was somewhat irrelevant to all of this. It might have been the catalyst for their meeting, but their relationship now existed in a way that was totally outside the bounds of the plan Lottie and she had discussed before Jane had met Zeus.

Anything important about her, she'd told him. She'd shared herself with him. And yet, he seemed determined to keep parts of himself closed off, even from her.

Was it possible that she was mistaking their physical intimacy for something more?

Lottie always said Jane was messed up because of the way her parents had treated her, and she knew her best friend was right. All her life, she'd known that her parents didn't love her like parents should love their child. They'd sent her away to boarding school at five years old, and from then on, she'd seen them only briefly during holidays, and sometimes, not even then. When Jane had started dating Steven and professed herself in love with him, Lottie had laughed and shaken her head. 'You want to be in love with him, because you want him to love you back. No one is going to fill that hole in here, though, that your parents dug, except for you. You have to love and accept yourself before anyone else can.'

Well, she'd been right about Steven, and she'd probably been right about all of it.

Now Jane was looking at Zeus as though he were in some way a mythical piece of her that had been missing all this time. Whereas she was probably just trying to fill that same awful, painful void. Not with love, but with intimacy and trust. Yes, the kind of trust she'd never known, because she sure as hell couldn't have said she felt that for her parents. And the fact he wouldn't open up to her showed that he didn't trust her, even after all she'd shared with him.

It hurt.

It hurt way more than a casual week-long fling should be able to hurt her. But Jane found, as she showered alone, that there was nothing she could do to change that. She wanted more from Zeus than he seemed willing to give, and she had two choices: accept it, or leave early. She didn't like either alternative.

CHAPTER TEN

'You're quiet,' he said as their dinner plates were cleared away. He'd sat through the meal, watching Jane push her quinoa salad around on her plate and take minuscule bites of the chargrilled fish, occasional sips of wine. It wasn't like she'd been sulking. Nor ignoring him. She'd asked questions about his grandparents, as well as the history of the area, but there was a tension in her that was very, very obvious. In complete contrast to the way she'd been in the water that very afternoon.

Before he'd joined her and shut down her line of questioning.

Because she asked too much. No, she *saw* too much. Other women had asked him personal questions, and he'd never found it hard to sidestep them. With Jane, he felt a pull towards full disclosure, and it made him uncomfortable. Hell, it made him want to break out in a cold sweat. His one rule in life was not to trust *anyone*. Or anything. He dealt in facts, figures, the tangible certainty of black-and-white numbers. When it came to people, he expected to be disappointed. To get hurt.

'I'm tired,' she said, pulling her lips to the side. Lying. She was upset. Uncertain.

'Jane,' he said on a tight sigh, because he knew why she was upset now; he just wasn't sure how to broach it.

He didn't have to worry about that.

'Zeus, I've never done anything like this before,' she said after a beat, her voice a little uneven. 'As you know.' Those words were slightly acerbic. 'I don't really know how it's meant to work.'

He stared at her. 'Work?'

'Yeah. Like, is it just sex? Is that the main thing we're doing?'

His gut churned. Wasn't that his stock in trade? How he usually had relationships? Sure, there was the polite dinner beforehand, a bit of surface-level conversation, but ultimately, he preferred to keep things easy. Casual. Enjoyable.

'You're upset.'

'I'm trying to understand,' she corrected with a defiant tilt of her chin, 'how you expect me to be.'

'I just want you to be yourself,' he muttered, recognising the hypocrisy of that. As did she, evidently, because she sat back in her chair and crossed her arms, one brow arching upwards.

'Are you sure? Because when I'm myself, and I try to ask you questions, you shut me down.'

She had a point, but she was also being a little unreasonable.

'I spoke to you about my mother today.'

'And it was like pulling teeth.'

'What do you want? A therapy session? Would you like me to bare my soul to you?'

'Not if you don't want to,' she snapped, reaching for

her wine and taking a sip before replacing it on the table with enough force to slosh the liquid against the edges of the glass like a roiling ocean.

'I don't want to,' he said, wishing the words sounded slightly less accusatory.

'Fine, then. So, it's just sex.'

But that characterisation sat ill in his gut. 'Jane—'

'No, it's fine. It's just good for me to know, so I can personally do a little less of the soul baring.'

He ground his teeth. 'I didn't mean that.'

'This is my problem, not yours.'

'What problem?'

'Nothing.'

'Jane—'

'It doesn't matter.' She stood up and paced towards the railing, turning her rigid, straight back to him, staring out in the direction of Crete. He looked at her for several beats before pushing back his own chair and striding in her direction.

She whirled around as he approached. 'I don't want to talk about it.'

She was hurting. He'd hurt her. He shook his head, unable to accept that. 'I'm sorry.'

She glanced away. 'Don't.'

'This is different. Everything's different with you. I don't know what I'm doing, either.'

That had her eyes slamming back to his with a ferocity that almost knocked him backwards.

'What do you mean?'

'You've been making conversation, asking questions about me, my life. That's fine. You're not the first woman to be curious.' Her cheeks flushed pink. 'But you are the first woman I've ever felt like I wanted to be honest with. To actually *talk* to. Not as a means to an end, but because there's something addictive about you. And that scares the hell out of me, Jane.'

'Scares you?' she repeated, her eyes on him like he was a puzzle she desperately wanted to break.

'I don't like things in my personal life to be unpredictable.'

She frowned, her features shifting, softening. 'Because of your mother?'

His first instinct was to deny it. He *hated* to discuss any of it. He'd built walls around his pain, and he liked having those walls there. They kept him safe, secure, able to function in the world. Because deep down, he knew that nine-year-old he'd once been was still a part of him, reeling from the very idea that his mother, the woman he loved more than anyone on earth, could possibly be so sick.

How could he deny it to Jane, though? Because it wasn't just his mother. His father had further pulled the rug out from under him with the revelation of his infidelity and secret child. The sense of betrayal was immense.

'I don't trust easily,' he said after a beat. 'And yet, I find myself wanting to trust you, Jane. Why is that?'

Her eyes widened and her skin paled, almost as if it was the last thing she expected—or wanted—him to say. 'I don't know.' A whisper, and then she reached for his hand. 'But it's something we have in common. I mean, after Steven, trusting anyone has been almost impossible for me, but with you…'

His eyes closed on a wave of acceptance. So, it was different, for both of them.

'I get that you find it hard to open up to people, but you just lost your mother, Zeus. That's got to bring up some issues. I'm just saying I'm here.'

For the next week, anyway. 'I know,' he said with a single nod. 'And thank you.'

Jane wasn't sure he should be thanking her. Not after she'd lost her temper, all because of his perfectly reasonable desire to maintain some personal distance between them. She'd felt lost, though, confused, worried that she was yet again feeling more for someone than she should. And wasn't she?

I don't trust easily, and yet I find myself wanting to trust you, Jane.

In the middle of the night, with Zeus fast asleep beside her, she slipped out of bed and moved from their room, out onto the deck. It was an inky-black night with low cloud cover, meaning the stars were covered and those that weren't were dimmed by the light pollution of Crete. Nonetheless, she settled back onto the large pool lounger they'd shared that first night and stared upwards, as though answers would come to her if only she looked long enough. Except they didn't, perhaps because there was no satisfying answer.

Instead, she lifted her phone and tapped out a message to Lottie.

How's it going?

'Couldn't sleep?' Zeus's voice was a deep rumble and Jane jumped, guilty at having been sending a message to Lottie—the woman who single-handedly wanted to bring about Zeus's removal from his family business.

'Nope.'

'Funny, I thought you'd have been worn out,' he teased, coming to sit beside her, sliding an arm around her and drawing her to his chest. She nuzzled in there, sighing at how right it felt to be this close to him, how much she loved it here.

'Oh, you're doing an excellent job in that department. Don't worry, Mr Papandreo.'

'Are you still upset?' he asked after a slight pause.

She glanced up at his face, her heart turning over in her chest. She shook her head.

'What did you mean earlier, when you said this is your problem, not mine?'

Jane's stomach clenched. 'Oh. It doesn't matter.'

'Now who's avoiding the difficult questions?' he asked, squeezing her shoulder lightly.

Her smile was half-hearted but then she sighed, resting in closer to his side, her hand absent-mindedly drawing spirals around his hip area. 'I'm not close to my parents,' she said, and if he thought it was a strange comment, he didn't say anything. 'Not like it sounds as though you were with your mother and are with your father.'

She felt him shift a little, and sympathy tightened in her gut. Did he know about his father's affair? Or was it multiple affairs? There was so much Jane didn't know, and yet the small amount of information she had about the other man made her angry. On behalf of Lottie, yes, but now also on behalf of Zeus.

'*Are* you close with your father?' she asked, tilting her face to his.

'It's complicated.' He'd said that earlier today, too, when she'd asked about his relationship with Aristotle.

'In what way?'

But he stiffened perceptibly. 'We were talking about your parents,' he reminded her, and a familiar sense of irritation sparked inside her chest. She didn't push it, though. She'd told him how she felt, and now it was up to Zeus to change, or not. She knew that this was new for him, though, that he was grappling with the new experience of how much he wanted to confide in her, and that had to be enough.

'When I say we're not close, I mean… I barely have a relationship with them.'

He was very quiet, but his eyes were intensely focused on her face.

'I was sent away to boarding school when I was very young, and I spent most of my time there. In the holidays, I would go home, and sometimes my parents were there, sometimes they weren't. Usually, it was a nanny who had the most to do with me.'

He spoke soft and low, 'I see.'

'My father's job required him to travel a lot. My mother went with him. They never planned to have children. I was a mistake.'

'An accident,' he corrected, as though the semantics of that might save her from the pain of knowing how unwanted she'd been.

'I think my mother did her best for a few years, but she grew tired of it all. Hence, boarding school.'

He shook his head a little. 'Were you at least happy there?'

She laughed, but a sound without humour. 'I hated it. I was teased mercilessly in primary school.'

'What about?' he demanded with a sense of outrage that softened parts of her she hadn't known needed it.

'Promise you won't laugh?'

He nodded gravely.

'My name.'

'Jane?'

'My name is actually Boudica,' she muttered. 'My parents, it turns out, decided to burden me with that, too. It wasn't enough for me to know I wasn't wanted, why not throw a truly unusual name into the mix?'

'I like it,' he said, and her heart turned over in her chest. 'It's beautiful.'

'I hated it.' She didn't go into the nicknames. 'And it was different. Too different for the children at school to understand.'

'It's just a name.'

'You know what kids are like. Once they got it into their heads to tease me about that, and saw they could get a reaction, they found other things.' She glanced downwards, self-conscious at revealing this to him. 'Anyway, thank God when I changed schools, they actually moved me back down, closer to London. I didn't know anyone. It was a proper fresh start. And on the first day, I met my best friend, Lottie, and that changed everything.' She realised, only after she'd finished talking, that she'd probably revealed way too much. What if he knew his half-sister's name was Lottie? What if he knew she'd gone to a boarding school on the outskirts of London?

But there was no recognition on his face, only a mix of sympathy and curiosity. 'How?'

She expelled a shaking breath of relief. 'Lottie was just like me, in lots of ways. Her own childhood was pretty messed up. She wasn't super close to her mother or father. We just got each other. But she's different to me in one vital way.'

'Oh?'

'She's as tough as nails. Lottie's a fighter. She was just born that way. Or maybe life turned her into one? I don't know. But all the things that had happened to me and made me kind of timid and nervous had made her angry, determined to change the world. Lottie can't help but see a problem and want to fix it.'

'And you were something she wanted to fix?'

'She would say I didn't need fixing, that I just needed to understand myself better.'

Zeus's features shifted with admiration. 'Smart woman.'

Jane's chest spasmed. If only he *knew* that they were discussing his half-sister! Who was smart, and kind and just generally wonderful!

'Oh, yes, and my biggest champion. She just had a way of making me see sense.' Jane moved her hand to his, lacing their fingers together. 'So, when I started dating Steven, and told Lottie I was in love, she took it with a grain of salt. She understood what I definitely wasn't able to—that I was looking for the kind of love and acceptance I'd always wanted and never got. My being needy didn't make Steven any more likely to love nor deserve me.' Another sigh. 'I wish I'd listened to her. Lottie would have never trusted a guy like him.'

'You weren't to blame,' he said firmly, as if it was the most important thing in the world that she understands that.

'I know. But at the same time, Lottie is just so much better at this stuff.'

'Despite what you think, Jane, you're trusting. That's not a weakness. Even after your parents' neglect, you see the best in people.'

Her lips pulled to the side as she considered that. 'Why can't you do that?'

He stared down at her, surprised by her having turned it back on him.

'You have seen your mother suffer for a long time—it's impacted you. I do understand that. But why can't you accept that grief is a part of life, in the same way joy is, and that you can't have one without the other?'

A muscle jerked low in his jaw; he didn't answer.

Jane settled back against his chest. 'Tell me about her,' she said quietly, because in asking about his mother, she wasn't asking him to recount his experiences of her illness, or her death, but rather her life. And she listened as he—reluctantly at first, and then more willingly—began to describe her. Her likes, her hobbies, her passions, the food she'd made for him when he came home from school, all of it. At some point, they drifted off to sleep like that, her head on his chest, her mind and heart filled with his words, the spectre of his mother over them, like an angel of destiny.

The next day, the boat moved to a different island, this one smaller and covered in greenery, so they walked a nature path from one side to the other and stopped for lunch at a small, beachfront taverna that served the crispiest, saltiest potatoes Jane had ever eaten. They drank ice-cold beer, then walked back towards the boat, and whatever frustrations Jane had felt the day before, about the parts of himself that Zeus kept walled off, seemed to have ebbed away like the waves in the ocean. Perhaps because he *had* started to talk to her the night before. Or perhaps because he'd acknowledged his shortcomings and the reasons for them. Or maybe because he'd told her that she was different, special, and she was still, deep down, that same seventeen-year-old, wanting to be loved.

Her step faltered slightly as that idea burst into her mind.

Loved?

It wasn't about love. Not with Zeus. Making love, sure. Passion. Pleasure. Respect. She enjoyed his company.

But she couldn't—wouldn't—love him.

How impossibly complicated, not to mention outrageously stupid, would that be? This was the man who'd been—admittedly unwittingly—an instrument of Lottie's pain all her life. How often had they stared daggers at him, whenever there'd been a photo of Zeus and Aristotle attending an event together? Lottie, glutton for punishment that she was, had set up a news alert on her phone and got emailed any time Aristotle or Zeus were mentioned, so there was never a shortage of information to devour and despise.

Like a good best friend, or an excellent foot soldier dragooned into a war out of loyalty alone, she'd hated Zeus, too. She'd hated Aristotle more, because his choices had wounded both Lottie and her mother, Mariah, but Zeus had committed the unforgivable crime of having held the place in life that should have been Lottie's. Whereas Lottie had had to live with the ignominy of knowing that her very existence was a burden and a regret, that she was so shameful to the Papandreos her mother had been paid millions of pounds to keep quiet.

Never mind that Aristotle had been the love of Mariah's life, and her heart had been broken beyond repair by his cruelty. Never mind that her heart had been too badly broken to properly accept her daughter into it.

It was just such an awful mess.

Even knowing all that, though, Jane couldn't bring herself to hate Zeus like she once had. She couldn't bring herself to think of him with anything other than...*not love*. She couldn't be stupid enough to make that mistake again. It had been bad enough with Steven, but at least then she'd had the defences of youth and naivety on her side. Now what?

She'd come into this with her eyes wide open.

She knew more than enough about him, and his predilection for short-term, meaningless flings. And she knew all the emotional baggage—even if he didn't—that made any kind of real relationship between them impossible.

So why did she walk with him, hand in hand, on that small island in the south of Greece, and smile as though she was the happiest woman in the world? She smiled, she realised, like a woman in love—apparently, some parts of her just hadn't quite gotten the memo.

CHAPTER ELEVEN

Long, sun-drenched days bled into balmy, starlit nights, all of them spent either in the water, on ancient, stunning islands, or naked together on the boat. Of all the weeks in her life, Jane had never known one to go as swiftly as this one. It was as though time had been sped up, and they both sensed it. They slept sparingly, catching a few hours here or there, when they were too utterly exhausted to fight it any longer.

They ate the most beautiful food, whether on the islands they visited, or aboard the boat. Zeus's chef procured just-caught seafood, the ripest fruit and vegetables, and served it all simply, to showcase the delightful flavours.

And they talked. Not about Zeus's mother, or his father, or Jane's parents, but about their lives, their childhoods, their favourite movies, books, places they'd visited. They made each other laugh in a way that Jane knew she could become addicted to, if she weren't very, very careful.

So, she was careful.

Careful not to let her guard down completely. Careful not to let her heart be exposed more than it had been.

Careful not to fantasise about falling in love with a man such as Zeus. Or Zeus himself, more specifically, because she doubted that there was another man like him.

But two days before she was due to leave, as they were walking along a deserted beach at sunset, he stopped walking all of a sudden and spun Jane around, so that she was looking out to sea. He pulled her back against his chest, held her there, so her breath grew rushed and hot.

'Do you see that mountain over there, in the distance?'

She squinted across the sea, to where a shape seemed to emerge from the middle of the ocean. 'Yeah?'

'That's Prásino Lófo,' he said.

She repeated the Greek words before tilting her face to his. 'What does it mean?'

'Very literally, it means Green Hill,' he said with a slow smile.

'Green Hill. Erm...very...er...creative.'

'The name came with the island.' He shrugged. 'My grandfather bought it, as a gift for my *yaya*.'

Her smile slipped and she refocused her attention on the island itself. She couldn't see much of it, but she tilted her face to his.

'It's your family's island?'

'When my parents married, my grandparents gave it to them as a wedding present.'

Jane nodded, but her mind was galloping ahead, even before he spoke the words.

'It has always been promised to me, when I marry,' he said. 'It's tradition.'

When he marries.

Someone else.

A reality that was far closer than Jane dared to think about. She couldn't. She wouldn't.

'Some wedding present,' she said, the words rushed and a little high-pitched. 'I thought crystal bowls were the norm.'

'Or candlesticks,' he responded, squeezing her tighter around the waist.

'Or at least registering for gifts. And I don't think you could put a Greek island on your registry without people thinking you were a little touched in the head. Then again, perhaps in the circles you move in...' She let the sentence taper off because she had no way of finishing it. She didn't want to contemplate Zeus marrying, belonging—in the sense that any human could belong to another—to someone else. Coming home to her, holding her, kissing her, making love to her.

Jane squeezed her eyes shut, her back to him, before forcing the thoughts from her mind.

'What's it like?'

'I haven't been there in years,' he admitted. 'But I remember it as being quite beautiful.'

They began to walk once more.

'It's overgrown and lush, with forests from one side to the other, though my father did add a very nice home and a nine-hole golf course.'

'As one does,' Jane drawled, earning an indulgent smile from Zeus.

'He stopped going there, once my mother was too ill to travel.'

'It must have been so hard on you both,' she murmured.

And perhaps because their time together was drawing to a close, he glanced down at her and said, 'It was, at first. I didn't know how to handle it. Seeing her like that. She'd always been so vibrant, so alive. And then she got sick, and the treatments were worse than the cancer. She slept almost all the time. I couldn't go near her in case I had a cold or flu. It was almost impossible to understand, as a boy. All I wanted was to be able to click my fingers and make her well.'

'Oh, Zeus,' she said, shaking her head a little.

'I spent a lot of time with my grandparents. They were very good at trying to keep everything as normal as possible for me, but I knew. I knew how sick she was, and that there was nothing I could do to help her.'

She squeezed his hand.

'I hated it, *agapeméni*. I hated feeling as though I was powerless to do a damned thing. Seeing her in pain, my father heartbroken, my whole world slipped through my fingers. I could do nothing.'

She shook her head, tears threatening. 'That's not true. You were there, for your father, and your mother. You stepped in and helped with the business, you read her stories, you grew into the kind of man she must have desperately hoped you would be. She would have been so proud of you, Zeus. She got to see you become this.' She squeezed his hand again, in the hope it would show him how much she meant it.

'I think she would have liked to see me take a different path than this.'

'In what way?'

He was quiet for several long strides, and then, on a long exhalation, 'From a very young age, the company became my entire life. At first, it was an interest, a passion rather than anything else. But as she became more and more sick, it became a tangible distraction. Somewhere I could go and be useful. I had no power to heal my mother, but with the company, I was able to do *something*. I was good at it, too. I stepped into my father's shoes. I saw problems and I fixed them. I saw opportunities and took them. I became obsessed and gradually, it became my whole life.'

Something hard and sharp opened up inside Jane. A shape that was almost impossible to accommodate, and every step she took seemed to jag it against her ribcage.

'But it's just a business,' she said eventually, the words a little breathless. 'And isn't the point of business to make money? Clearly, you have enough money.' She sounded desperate to her own ears.

'Money is the last thing I care about,' he contradicted.

'Then why does it matter so much?' She couldn't meet his eyes. She couldn't look at him without the dark, all-consuming sense of betrayal rearing up and swallowing her alive. Lottie was going to take the business from him. She was going to move heaven and earth to achieve that—anyone who knew Lottie knew that she always, always achieved what she set her mind to. And Zeus was going to lose *everything*.

'Where do I begin?' he said with a lift of one shoulder. 'It gave me a sense of control. When things at home were spinning wildly away from me, and I could do nothing to help, in the business, I could pull levers to effect change. It was my sense of purpose when I needed one most. My mother's death hasn't changed that. If anything, it makes me more determined to build the Papandreo Group into the best it can be.'

Jane lifted a hand to her lips, pressing it there. The telltale gesture simply slipped out, but Zeus didn't appear to notice.

'When I took over as group CEO, I came up with a ten-year plan that would revolutionise our business model. I'm only five years in, but already we're tracking well ahead of schedule.'

'Your father must be very proud,' she murmured, simply to fill the silence, because he had told her something great about himself, and she needed to acknowledge it. But her head was spinning, her heart hurting, her chest heavy, as though bags of cement had been placed on her.

'My father...' He hesitated and she glanced up at him, seeing tension radiating from his handsome face. 'We're not in a good place right now.'

She could tell how hard it was for Zeus to admit that. It was the sharing of a secret, of a part of him that he instinctively wanted to keep hidden.

Everything she knew about Aristotle caused her to dislike the older man, but she kept her tone neutral as she asked, 'Why not?'

Zeus's eyes skimmed to her face then bounced away to the ocean. They were close to where his boat was moored, but she didn't want to leave this idyllic beach without finishing this conversation. She was worried that once they stepped onboard, he'd move on to something else. She slowed her step imperceptibly.

Zeus made a gruff sound, part sigh, part grimace. 'He's not the man I thought he was.'

Jane chewed into her lower lip. This was getting close to home, close to Lottie, she just knew.

'Last week he told me that he'd had an affair.'

Jane's footing stumbled a little and Zeus's arm shot out to wrap around her waist. Instinctively protective. Her heart sped up.

'Recently?' Her voice was hoarse to her own ears.

'Who knows? This affair was many years ago, but how can I trust it hasn't been going on longer? That there haven't been other women?'

'Why would he tell you about one but not others?' she pointed out, logically.

'Because in this instance, there's a complication.' He glanced down at her and Jane's heart skipped several beats in a row. 'A daughter.'

She gasped. Lottie. So, Zeus had only just found out about her. He hadn't known about Lottie and chosen to ignore her. He'd been as innocent in all of this as Lottie herself. Guilt, grief, pain and panic swirled inside Jane's gut.

'I see,' she whispered, because she *did* see. She saw all too much.

'She's twenty-three, and my father has been supporting her all these years. While my mother lay dying…'

'What would you have had him do, Zeus?' she felt compelled to say, in defence of her best friend. 'Leave her to fend for herself?'

A muscle jerked in Zeus's jaw.

'He took steps to make sure she was never discovered—for my mother's sake. It would have destroyed her to know he'd cheated.'

Jane's eyes filled with tears; she blinked quickly to dispel them.

'But now my mother's gone, and all of a sudden, he wants to acknowledge this woman. To bring her into the family,' Zeus spat, and now Jane found the simple act of walking beyond her.

'What?' Her voice was hoarse. Just a whisper.

Zeus was so wrapped up in his own thoughts that he evidently didn't notice how pale Jane had become, all the colour fading from her cheeks as she stared up at him.

'As if I have any interest in knowing her.'

'Why not?' Jane groaned, pressing a hand to his chest. This was *Lottie* they were talking about. Lottie, Jane's best friend. Lottie, who was smart and charming and sweet and kind. Lottie, who could light a room up just by walking into it.

'She is evidence of my father's failings.'

Jane's eyes swept shut. 'Zeus, it's not that simple.'

He was silent.

Jane tried again. 'She's a person, and none of this is her fault, just as it's not your fault. And maybe it's not your father's fault, either. He made a bad decision when your mother got sick. A terrible decision, but he was probably driven half-mad with grief and worry. People do silly things sometimes. They make mistakes. Surely, you have it in your heart to forgive him?'

'No.' He stared down at her now with eyes that were black with fierce determination, and she shivered; this was a side to him Jane hadn't seen. 'Betrayal is the one thing I cannot forgive, not from someone I trust.'

Jane's heart turned to ice and her skin stung all over. Panic flared through her.

'The worst of it is because of the way our company is structured, she has it in her power to take it away from me. All of it.' The words were clipped, his tone short. A lump formed in Jane's throat. 'I can't let that happen.'

She wanted to agree with him. If she didn't know Lottie, she would have readily nodded and told him that of course he couldn't. She knew what the company meant to Zeus; she understood why it was so special to him.

'Surely, you can work out a way to incorporate her into your life, your company...' Though she doubted Lottie would want that. It was all so useless.

'You cannot be serious?' His face held that same expression, that ruthless, bitter anger, so Jane flinched a little.

He softened immediately, lifting a hand to her cheek.

'You see goodness in everyone. I see only the risk of what could go wrong by involving the wrong person. Just because my father had an affair over two decades ago doesn't mean I have any interest in bonding with the woman he insists on calling my *sister*. As for the business, it is mine, Jane, and I will do whatever I can to ensure it stays that way.'

Jane spun away from him before he could see the heartbreak on her face, because she knew what it would take for him to secure the business. As soon as she left, he'd find someone to propose to and would marry as swiftly as the laws would allow. He would be someone else's husband, and Jane would be alone, licking her wounds, having failed Zeus and her best friend.

Only, later that night, back on the boat, Jane realised that maybe she could do something to fix this, after all. When she'd come to Greece, it had been with a simplistic and ill-thought-out plan to delay Zeus's marriage plans. To complicate things for him. She wasn't even sure *how* they'd thought she'd do that. It had been a knee-jerk reaction to the news Lottie had received about the company. Years and years of her hurt at having been hidden away by Aristotle Papandreo, paid off to stay silent, had culminated in a fierce, angry plan to make them pay.

But now Jane knew so much more. She'd seen behind the curtain, and she understood Zeus so much better. She understood his heart, his mind, his goodness and decency. What if she could convince Lottie to abandon her plans to take over the company, to force them into a meeting?

Zeus would never forgive her, Jane recognised. Her betrayal would make that impossible—he'd said as much, and she couldn't blame him. But so what? If it meant the two people she loved most—and she could no longer deny that she had fallen in love with him—could be made happy, could be united, then wasn't it worth sacrificing her own happiness?

Wasn't that her duty?

When you loved, you did what was right for the person you loved, even if it hurt.

And it would hurt, she recognised. It would hurt like the devil, but she would do it. Just as soon as this week was over, she'd fly to Lottie and she'd convince her—she'd use every last word in the dictionary until Lottie understood that Zeus was not the monster they'd always built him up to be. He was, in every way, the total opposite.

When the sun came up the next morning, there was a heaviness inside Jane. It was their last day together. After this, everything between them would change. As soon as she forced a meeting between the two half siblings—which she now knew she absolutely must move heaven and earth to accomplish—Zeus would know that she'd been lying to him all along and he would never again look at her with eyes that seemed to promise he'd climb into heaven and pick out the stars if she asked it of him.

She sat up groggily in the bed, looking towards the window to see a lot of trees on the shore of a sweet little cove. The boat must have moored here overnight; she could hardly keep track of all the islands they'd hopped to.

'I thought we could take a look up close,' he said. 'Start getting your land legs back.'

She glanced down at Zeus, who was awake, but reclined in the same pose he'd been in a moment ago, his bare chest exposed to her, his face so sharply angular and beautiful. She took a moment to commit this to memory and to fold the memory in a little space inside her brain.

'What is it?'

'Prásino Lófo.'

'Your family's island?'

He nodded.

'I'd love to see it,' she said, though the words were heavy, because she knew what the island meant to him and his family. If her plan to unite Lottie and Zeus didn't work, then the marriage wars would be back on, and this island would be Zeus's gift from his father. To enjoy with his new bride.

Bitterness soured her mouth.

'We'll have lunch there,' he said, his hand reaching out for her waist and pulling her towards him, oblivious to her inner turmoil. 'There's no need to rush—we have plenty of exploring we can do here first.' He kissed her as though he had not a care in the world. As though the walls weren't all coming crashing down around them. And, Jane supposed, for him, they weren't. This was still just a simple week-long fling. She surrendered to his touch, his kiss, to the feelings he could evoke, partly because they drove the guilt from her mind temporarily, but mostly because she simply couldn't—and didn't want to—resist him.

He was taunting himself, and he knew it. Bringing Jane to this island so he could always imagine her here. Jane, who might have been his perfect, ideal wife, in a parallel universe. In a universe where he could open himself up to the uncertainties of life, to the idea of loving someone who might leave him, who might hurt him.

In that world, she belonged here.

In this world, too, he thought, watching as she strolled onto the large timber balcony that hung, cantilevered, from the house, over a cliff atop the ocean. 'It's so beautiful,' she said, shaking her head a little, so her blond hair, naturally wavy, he'd discovered this week, flew loose around her face, reminding him of gold.

'It was a labour of love for my parents,' Zeus admitted, remembering the way they'd pored over the plans when his mother was well enough. 'They would talk about coming here with their grandchildren.' His smile was grim. They'd all known his mother wouldn't live to see grandchildren, particularly when marriage had been the last thing on Zeus's mind. But it had given her pleasure to imagine, to hope.

'Hence the millions of bedrooms?' Her tone was teasing as she came to stand beside him. 'You'd better get busy, Zeus, because there's room here for at least ten children.'

He didn't laugh. The thought of marrying someone else, of having children with them, was now like acid inside his throat all the time.

'Do you think you will?' She glanced up at him, the humour gone from her face, too.

He didn't follow. 'Have ten children?'

She waved a hand in the air, her features a little troubled. 'Marry.'

He shifted his body to face her, and the air between them seemed to grow heavy and thick all at once, making it difficult to breathe. In another world, if he were any other man, this might be where he'd say something like, *That depends if you'll agree to marry me.* But Zeus had been shaped by all that he'd seen and lost, by the fear and pain and anticipation of death that he'd been forced to live with almost his entire life. The thought of opening himself up to that again was the antithesis of his approach to life.

And yet, the thought of Jane hearing about his engagement in the papers in a week's time, maybe two weeks, depending on how quickly he acted, and not understanding his reasons for it...

'When I marry,' he said carefully, 'it will be a pragmatic marriage, not for love.'

She bit into her lip, her eyes showing a swirling current of emotion. 'Why?'

'Because I don't want that kind of marriage.'

She shook her head. 'That doesn't make sense.'

'Doesn't it?' He reached out and caught her hair, tucking it behind her ear. 'You know me, Jane.' Even to his own ears, his voice was deep and rumbly. 'After this week, I think you know me better than anyone. Can you really stand there and tell me you don't understand?'

Her lips parted on a quick expulsion of breath.

'The more I felt for someone,' he said, voice gruff, as though it had been dragged from his chest over hot coals, 'the less able I would be to have them in my life.' He stroked her cheek. 'I'd always rather let go on my terms, you see.'

Did she understand what he meant? What he wasn't saying? Did she know how much she'd come to mean to him?

A single tear slid down her cheek, and she turned her face into his palm, eyes sweeping shut. The afternoon sun dipped towards the ocean and cast her in a halo of gold, so she shimmered like an angel.

'I'll always be glad to have met you,' he said, and

then, because he couldn't resist, he pulled her to his body and kissed her as though they'd just said their wedding vows, and this was the beginning of the rest of their lives together, rather than the beginning of the end—their last night.

CHAPTER TWELVE

On the morning of their final day together, Zeus woke early, despite the fact they'd barely slept. Urgency had overtaken them both, so they'd made love hard and fast and then long and slow, reaching for each other, memorising every inch of one another's bodies, remembering everything about this connection they shared.

But the morning broke and with it the reality that Jane would leave him today.

He'd known it was coming.

They'd faced that reality together a week ago, and here they now were, staring down the barrel of the End. He refused to let that hurt him. Or to admit how much it was hurting him?

He wanted to stay with her, in bed, but at the same time, he was possessed by a strange energy. An adrenaline that was pumping through his veins, making him jumpy and unsettled, so he stepped out of the bed with one last look at her sleeping frame, her hair over one shoulder, her lips parted in sleep, and his heart seemed to splinter into a thousand pieces.

Lips a grim line, he strode from the room towards the galley, where he began to brew a coffee, staring out at Prásino Lófo with a heavy heart. Jane had belonged here; he wasn't imagining that. When she'd stepped onto the island the day before, he'd felt as though something in his chest had locked into place, and that feeling had only built and built until he couldn't help but imagine her there forever. His wife, his other half, his love.

He dropped his head and stared at the benchtop, his heart racing now, a fine bead of perspiration forming at the nape of his neck, because he could no longer pretend that he didn't love her. That he didn't trust her. That he didn't want her—not just out of a sense of transient limerence, but in a lasting, vital way.

It terrified him, because *nothing* was lasting. Nothing was certain.

He'd learned that lesson at a very, very young age. He'd lived alongside a permanent fear of waking up, every day, and having it be the last day in which he saw his mother. That uncertainty had damned near eaten him alive, and he'd seen it all but destroy his father.

How could Zeus possibly be stupid enough to have allowed himself to fall in love?

He had to let Jane go. He had to say goodbye, watch her walk away and never, ever think of her again. He had to employ every ounce of strength at his disposal. Only then would he be safe from those exact same feelings.

Waking up, not knowing if she would be safe, if she would be well. He couldn't do it again, not ever. Loving Jane would mean forever putting his heart on the line, making himself vulnerable and weak. He couldn't do it.

Except...

Would Jane's leaving solve anything? Whether or not

he loved her was not an academic concept, but rather, he now accepted, reality. He did love her. She was a part of him, body and soul. So that vulnerability was there, whether she was in his life or not.

The foolish part of what he'd done was inviting her on the boat. He should have run a mile in the opposite direction from her that very first night, when he'd kissed her and felt as if the world's rotation had dramatically picked up speed.

That was when he'd seen the warning signs, heard the siren, had known she'd be trouble. Had known she'd threaten the parameters of his existence. He hadn't run, though, at least, not away from her. If anything, he'd barrelled headlong into this regardless, and now, a little more than a week later, he was in love with her.

He was *in love* with her.

He lifted his head, focusing once more on the island, his heart hammering into his ribcage as realisation began to unfurl through him. He *loved* her. And if she loved him, maybe he could have his cake and eat it, too? He needed to get married, and he'd been thinking of his female friends who might be open to a businesslike marriage arrangement, but somehow, he'd found an option that was so much better.

He could propose to Jane.

Marry her.

Bring her here, to this island, where his wife belonged. Where *she* belonged. He could kiss her every day, for all the days of her life, so that she would never again feel unsafe or afraid. He could love her with every fibre of his being, accepting that risks were inherent to that, but that the alternative was so, so much worse.

Losing her by choice was an action he would never forgive himself for—if he let her walk away without telling her how he felt, he'd always regret it.

His heart burst with lightness and *joy*, an emotion he couldn't remember feeling much of before meeting Jane. It was as though she'd woken him up from a terrible and protracted nightmare, and he was remembering who he was again.

He spun around, intending to stride back to his cabin and wake her up with the realisation he'd just had, but he stopped, because she'd been up almost all night as well, and he didn't want to break her sleep. Yet.

He could wait.

He could wait, to deliver the most important words of his life.

Adrenaline continued to pump through his veins, making him jumpy. Coffee probably wasn't necessary, but he poured a cup anyway and idly picked up his phone, opening his emails—a habit he'd been neglecting since being boat-bound with Jane.

He couldn't help but grin as he flicked through them. Not because of the content, but because he had the woman of his dreams on the boat, a woman he trusted and loved in equal measure, and this was going to be the beginning of the rest of their lives together.

Near the top of his emails, he recognised one had finally come through from the UK-based detective he'd hired. Amazingly, Jane had even managed to push almost all thoughts of his *sister* from his mind.

He clicked into the email, and read the text:

Dear Mr Papandreo,

An extensive background check of Charlotte Shaw has now been conducted. Please find the following information:

Up until then, he hadn't even known her last name. It went on to list her date of birth, residential address, educational qualifications, the fact that she worked in the not-for-profit sector, and was not currently in a relationship.

Also, please find attached some photographs of the subject.

Should you require any further information, do not hesitate to reach out.

Zeus scrolled down to where the photos had loaded into the email. His finger was shaking slightly; he had no idea what she'd look like. She was his half-sister; his father's blood ran in her veins as surely as it ran through his, so he suspected she might look something like him, but the first image that came up on his phone showed a slender redhead with green eyes and alabaster skin. Only her expression was somehow familiar to him. It was a yearbook photo, probably taken sometime earlier, and she was staring directly at the camera in a 'don't mess with me' kind of way that he felt in his bones.

He scrolled to the next photo. This was taken more recently, by a telephoto lens, he'd guess, courtesy of the detective. Charlotte Shaw was stepping out of a grocery store, carrying a paper bag. He could just see the top of a baguette and a bottle of wine.

He flicked down to the next photo and froze. Or perhaps he didn't. Perhaps it was the whole world that froze? It didn't make sense. Nothing about it computed. What was his half-sister doing in a photograph with Jane Fisher? What was Jane—*his* Jane—doing with her arm around Charlotte Shaw's shoulders? The picture was taken from a newspaper, and the detective had cropped enough to show the headline, 'Breaking Barriers for a Cause.'

Perhaps they'd met through work. Met once. Didn't know each other.

But they didn't *look* like two people who didn't know each other. They looked...like friends. His heart thudded and acid burned the back of his throat as he began to look at Jane, and their relationship, through a wholly different prism. From their first meeting, at a bar he had been photographed leaving many, many times. If one did an internet search for his name and clicked into the images, he knew there were pictures there, clearly showing him and the name of the establishment. How easy it would be to find him—and how easy to tempt him, with someone like Jane.

His blood thundered and roared through his body, deafeningly loud.

He loaded up a search browser and typed in Jane's name, as well as his half-sister's, and the full article was one of the first to appear. It had only been written six months earlier.

Childhood best friends making waves in the not-for-profit sector, was the subtitle.

Childhood best friends.

Charlotte Shaw, his half-sister, was Lottie. Jane's Lottie. The best friend he'd praised and been inwardly glad Jane had in his corner!

Nausea rolled through him. Disbelief was quickly followed by shock, then acceptance. And then, finally, fury.

Fury because he'd been played. But to what end? A part of him wanted to cling to the fanciful notion that this was all some big, silly coincidence. Something they could laugh about together. After all, Jane was the woman he loved. A part of him wanted to hold fast to the dreams he'd started to walk towards, to the future he'd envisaged only minutes ago.

But Zeus was not one to run and hide.

Jane had lied to him, and he had to know why. Boxing away the love he felt for her, telling himself it was based on falsity and pretence, he sat at the table and stared straight ahead, ordering his thoughts, making a plan and waiting. For when Jane woke up, they'd have this conversation, and he wouldn't rest until he knew everything.

'Good morning,' she said, trying to hide her ambivalence about whether or not the morning was, in fact, good or not. Ambivalence? She wished she felt ambivalent. The truth was she knew this was going to be one of the hardest days of her life. The only thing getting her through was the certainty that she was leaving Zeus to fly to Lottie, whom she would sit down and make see sense about this whole situation. Just imagining the truce she could bring about between the two of them was almost enough to ease her pain. Almost, but not quite.

And maybe, just maybe, when it was all out in the open, and things had calmed down, Zeus might even understand...

'Are you packed?'

His voice was strange. Dark and heavy. His eyes met hers, but they were ice-cold, utterly different to how he'd looked at her the night before, with something that had felt almost like love to her silly wishful heart.

Perhaps he was just finding the emotion of the day too much, like she was? He was standing across the room, hips pressed to the kitchen counter, mug of coffee in hand, and he looked good enough to eat.

'I— Not yet.' She'd been putting it off, naturally. She wanted to eke out as much of this day together as she possibly could.

'I've organised for my helicopter to take you to Athens from the island. It will be ready in ten minutes.'

She gaped. 'Ten...minutes?'

He nodded once. 'Which should be just long enough for you to explain to me exactly how you know Charlotte Shaw, and exactly what the plan was in coming to Athens?'

Jane gasped, her eyes filling with stars, the world growing black, so for a fearsome moment she thought she might pass out. He was staring at her as though she were something disgusting on his shoe, as though he could barely stand to breathe the same air as her. 'How did you—?'

How he'd found out was hardly the most important thing to ask, but it was a reasonable question.

Nonetheless, his eyes flashed with fury that she'd immediately asked that, rather than something else.

'That's irrelevant. And I'll be the one posing the questions.'

She shuddered. He wasn't angry, she realised. She'd been wrong to perceive fury in his eyes. Disgust, yes, and coldness, which was somehow so, so much worse.

'You knew about the marriage clause of my family's business all along.'

She closed her eyes on a wave of panic. 'Zeus, let me explain—'

'Did you know about it?' he interrupted, staring her down, so when she blinked her eyes open, she was lanced by the intensity of his gaze.

'Yes.' A whispered admission; a death knell. His own eyes closed then, briefly, on a wave of acceptance, so she realised that up until that moment, he'd been holding out some form of hope that maybe she hadn't known. That maybe the marriage clause *wasn't* why she'd come to Athens.

'And you were supposed to, what? Tempt me into marriage then stand me up at the altar?'

'No.' She spat the word like a curse.

'I find that hard to believe.'

'It wasn't a particularly well-thought-out plan,' she whispered. 'Lottie—'

At the mention of Charlotte's abbreviated name, he cursed softly so she grimaced.

'She was upset. After your father told her about the arrangement, she...'

'Wanted the company, yes, that much I deduced for myself.'

'You see it as your birthright,' Jane murmured.

'It *is* my birthright. I was raised to do this.'

'But she is also a Papandreo.'

His nostrils flared.

Jane's loyalties were so incredibly torn. She had to make him see Lottie's side, even when she knew that would cost her everything with Zeus. Her throat hurt from the weight of unshed tears, but she continued.

'You don't know what it was like for her, Zeus.'

He made a gruff sound of disgust, but Jane continued regardless, her voice shaking a little. She felt tears splash down her cheeks, warm and fat, but she didn't bother to check them.

'All her life, Lottie has felt like someone people were ashamed of. Her mother—'

He swore again. 'Do *not* speak to me of that whore.'

'Zeus...' Jane was appalled. 'Mariah Shaw is *not* a whore, and I'll have you know she was head over heels in love with your father. She's loved him all this time, has never been with another man since. How can you possibly judge someone you've never met?'

A muscle jerked in his jaw as he continued to lance her with his dark stare.

'She didn't want to make things harder for him—'

'How generous of her.'

'Or your mother,' Jane added softly.

'And I'm sure the ten million pounds my father paid

her, not to mention ongoing child support, had nothing to do with that.'

Jane flinched on behalf of Lottie and her mother. 'You don't think Lottie was entitled to be raised in a lifestyle akin to yours? Would you have preferred it if your father had left Mariah to struggle, as a poor single mother?'

Zeus's face paled beneath his tan. At least on that front she was sure she'd gotten through to him.

'Five minutes,' he said, voice cold, so even if she had felt like she'd made some headway, she realised very quickly that it wasn't enough.

Jane closed her eyes, her heart hurting more than it had ever hurt in her life. 'What else do you want to know?'

'The plan. All of it.'

'There was no plan,' she said, but he made a scoffing noise to dispute that. 'Not a very good one, anyway.'

He stared at her, waiting for her to continue.

'Lottie wanted me to distract you,' she said, biting into her lip.

'To make me want you,' he murmured. 'So that I wouldn't propose to anyone else?'

Jane squeezed her eyes shut and nodded once, a tiny shift of her head.

'And in the meantime, she'd be looking for someone to get married to, so that she could take the business away from me?'

It all sounded so incredibly awful said like that. But what could she do? There was no sense denying it.

'Is that correct, Jane?'

She bit into her lip. 'You need to understand—'

His nostrils flared. 'I understand perfectly,' he cut her off. 'All this time, when you were imploring me to bare my soul to you, you already knew so much about me. You have *lied* to me, every step of the way, haven't you? From that first night in the bar, until this morning, you have hidden your true self from me.'

She shook her head, her stomach churning. 'No, Zeus, that's not true.' She strode across the room then, curling her hand around his arm, shaking him. She needed him to understand. 'Everything between us has been real. *This* is real.'

His only response was to angle his head and stare at her hand as though it were something vile and disgusting. 'Do not touch me, Jane.'

She dropped her hand like she'd been burned, quickly wiping away her tears, only for more to take their place.

'Zeus,' her voice trembled.

'You did so well,' he drawled. 'What excellent bait you proved to be. Though you didn't need to go so far as making up sob stories about your romantic past. I wouldn't have cared if you'd slept with every man in Britain—I still would have wanted you with the force of a thousand suns.'

'I didn't make that up,' she whispered, her chest cleaving apart at the very idea of lying about something so intimate. It had been such a huge deal for Jane to disclose the truth to him. She swallowed, but her throat was constricted. Her head ached.

'You'll forgive me if I don't believe you. You have no credibility with me, and with good reason, wouldn't you say?'

She was shaking like a leaf. She reached behind her for a chair, sitting down with a dull sense of aching bones.

'Unfortunately for you and your friend, your plan failed.'

Jane blinked up at him, eyes wide.

'I'm getting married, you see,' he said, and her heart stammered as her legs began to tremble.

'What?'

'Mmm-hmm. I proposed to a friend of mine the night I met you. You'll remember I had a dinner?'

Jane's lips parted.

'It was one of the reasons I had to bring you onto the boat. I could hardly risk the press getting wind of the fact I was sleeping with you, when my fiancée was off buying wedding clothes.'

'I don't believe you,' Jane whispered, shaking her head.

'Only one of us is a liar here, Jane.' The indictment was like a slap; she flinched at the depth of hatred in his voice. The ice. The rejection.

Every part of her hurt. Every cell, every drop of blood, every atom of her being.

'You think I haven't hated lying to you, Zeus?'

'You haven't exactly seemed conflicted.'

'Yeah, well, I have been,' she shouted, then sobbed, because it was all so awful, so devastatingly bad. 'Do you want to know what I was planning to do today?'

He stared back at her without asking the question.

'I was going to go to Lottie, to tell her about how wonderful you are, how much she'd love you if she got to know you. I was going to beg her to put off whatever plan she'd concocted and focus on meeting her half-brother, on meeting the man that I love.' Her voice stammered over the last word and her cheeks flushed with pink at what she was admitting to him. But he needed to know how real this was for her; how incredibly special it had all been.

'You don't love me,' he responded, rejecting her admission.

'How can you say that?'

'Because you have been lying to me this whole week,' he reminded her, voice deathly quiet.

She sobbed once more.

'I wanted to tell you the truth, but it's not my truth to tell. I needed Lottie…'

'You listened to me describe what that business means to me, all the while knowing that every moment we spent on this boat was a moment closer to your best friend triumphing over me, taking it all away.'

'I would have done everything in my power to stop that, I promise.'

'Your promises aren't worth a damned thing,' he snapped. 'Time's up.' He straightened, crossing his arms over his chest. 'I have a wedding to prepare for.'

She flinched, standing, moving to him, reaching out but he stepped away.

'Don't,' he insisted, firmly.

She could hardly speak for how hard she was crying. Her soul was shattered. Every part of her life had been distilled to this moment; she was falling apart.

'Please don't marry her,' she whispered.

He glared through her. 'You're trying to succeed in your plan, even now?'

She shook her head. 'I don't care about anything but this.' She pushed her hand into her chest then gestured to him. 'You and I—'

'Have been having sex,' he muttered.

'Don't do that.'

'Do what? Be honest? I'm sorry if that offends you.'

'Don't say we're just sex. You know this is so much more.'

'It's all a lie,' he spat. 'All of it.'

She wanted to scream at him, to make him understand how wrong he was, but what would the point be? He was clearly determined to think the worst. She sobbed and nodded, unable to think of a single thing she could say that might get through to him.

'I'm so sorry,' she whispered, because she was. From the very depths of her heart, she regretted having agreed to go along with this. And yet, if she hadn't, she never would have met Zeus, and she couldn't countenance that. 'And I do love you, Zeus. Whatever else you believe, I hope one day you'll at least accept that.'

And she turned and ran back to the room they'd been sharing, to throw her clothes into a bag so she could get off his boat before she collapsed into a heap.

CHAPTER THIRTEEN

FOR FORTY-EIGHT HOURS, Zeus did very little but drink Scotch, drift on the ocean in his yacht and contemplate every single word they'd spoken. Every emotion. Every barb. He'd accused her of lying—and she had—but he'd lied, too, in the end about his engagement. He was ashamed of himself for doing the one thing he'd promised them both he never would: he'd hurt her. And he'd done it deliberately. He'd wanted to dig the knife in, so to speak, because of how she'd made him feel.

So what? Didn't she deserve it?

Of course. She'd manipulated him for financial gain. She'd been sent by her best friend to destroy the one thing that mattered most to him. By every metric, she was an awful, awful person.

So why didn't he feel more relieved? Why was he drinking himself into a stupor rather than flying home and proposing to Philomena then and there?

Because he needed time to deal with this. Unlike his mother's death, he hadn't been braced for Jane's betrayal. He'd *trusted* her, he thought, angrily. He'd let his guard down with her, something he'd never done with another soul, and she'd promised him he could. That it was safe. She'd made him trust her. Because it wasn't enough just to screw with him? What kind of sick game had she wanted to play?

Disgust—at himself and her, at his father and Charlotte—flooded his body. He poured another measure of Scotch, held it close to his chest and tried to think clearly. To contemplate his next move. Marriage. To someone else. He knew it was vital, but just the thought of it turned his stomach.

He'd loved Jane, and despite her betrayal, there was a part of him that still did. At least, that loved the version of her she'd shown him.

This is real.

Liar.

He threw back the Scotch then slammed the glass down, wondering how the hell he could get her out of his head and heart.

Four days later, Zeus arrived at his office with no outward hint of what had happened on the boat. Dressed in a suit, he strode in, determined to take charge of his company, to work out a way to keep it in his name, telling himself that was still the most important thing in his life.

Only, within minutes of sitting behind his desk and drafting an email to his lawyer, one of his assistants buzzed his phone.

'I'm sorry to interrupt, sir, but there's a woman here to see you.'

Images of Jane filled his mind. Was it possible she was still here? That she'd come to see him? And so what if she had? His breath hitched in his throat. His gut shanked.

'I'm busy,' he replied, because it was important that he not see her again. Not yet. He wasn't prepared.

'She says it's urgent.'

He ground his teeth. 'Fine,' he said, standing. 'But tell her I only have five minutes.'

He prowled to his floor-to-ceiling window overlooking Athens and waited, every bone in his body feeling heavy and stiff. The door opened and he made an effort to turn slowly, to brace for the impact of seeing her.

It was not, however, Jane who'd come to his office, but rather the woman he'd spent weeks hating and despising. His half-sister, Charlotte Shaw.

'You,' he muttered, glaring at her, surprised that she was shorter in real life than he'd expected, and far slimmer, too.

'You,' she spat back at him, crossing her arms. 'Well, if I didn't hate you before, I sure as hell have a reason to now.'

He laughed darkly. 'Are you kidding me?'

'Nothing about this is remotely amusing.'

'You're telling me?' His eyes fell to her hand, and he saw on her ring finger a large emerald ring, so his stomach clenched—though, strangely, he'd been half expecting this, and he wasn't even sure he could raise the energy to care anymore. Ironic, given how focused he'd been a moment ago on securing the company. 'You're engaged?'

'And you're a Grade-A jackass,' she snapped.

His head reeled. 'You sent your best friend to Athens

to seduce me so you could steal my company,' he said baldly. 'And I'm the jackass?'

She at least had the decency to look ashamed.

'Yeah, well, you sent her home utterly destroyed, so what are you going to do about it?'

His gut churned. Pain slashed through him. Jane, destroyed. Like she'd been on the boat, when she'd sobbed and pleaded with him to understand that she loved him. When she'd apologised and said she wanted to explain, and he'd cut her off, because on that morning, he'd truly felt as though no explanation would ever suffice.

'I'm sure she'll recover.'

'Are you? Well, that shows how well you know her, because I've *never* seen Jane like this. Not even after Steven.' It was the worst thing Lottie could have said to him. The truth of that plunged into him like a knife.

'And it's my fault,' she continued. 'I'm the one who begged her to do this. I'm the one who pushed past her objections, who pleaded with her, because I knew that she would never say no to me. I used her,' Charlotte continued, guilt-stricken, crossing her arms, 'and now I have to fix it.'

'Some things can't be fixed,' he said darkly, thinking of his love for Jane and how transformative it had been—and how devastating to recognise that it had also been based on a scam.

'You're not even going to try?'

'Why would I?' he demanded, blanking Jane from his mind with Herculean effort.

'So, you don't love her?'

He kept his expression neutral, but just barely. 'I can't see what business that is of yours.'

'I'm making it my business.'

He actually laughed, a deranged sort of sound, totally lacking humour. 'That's not your prerogative.'

'This makes it so.' She lifted her hand, so the ring sparkled visibly. 'You care about this company.'

His nostrils flared with an angry breath.

'You want to keep it?'

He thrust a hand onto his hip.

'Well, I will walk away, sign whatever I need to in order to give up my stake in it, if you promise to at least go and *talk* to her.'

The bottom seemed to be tilting out of his world.

'I thought you wanted the company badly enough to do anything?'

'I want my best friend to be happy more,' she said with a withering and derisive scowl. 'I would give up anything for her, as she would for me. Did you even know that's what she was planning to do?'

He didn't move.

'She was coming home to tell me that she loved you, that she thought I'd love you, too, that she wanted us to be friends. She knew it might mean losing you, but she was going to put you and me first, because that's the kind of person she is. And if you truly don't see that,' she said, stalking back towards the door and wrenching it inwards, 'then you don't deserve her.' She left without a backwards glance and Zeus had the unfamiliar and unwelcome experience of having been hit by a tornado.

* * *

For the first time in a week, Jane left the flat. She didn't feel like it. In fact, she desperately wanted to stay buried under her mountain of duvets and keep crying, but there was also a restlessness to her grief, or perhaps to her cravings for Zeus, that had her yearning to move her body. To feel blood rushing through her, to feel *alive* once more. So, she pulled on yoga pants and a loose shirt and set out for a run, targeting her favourite route through the Heath, uncaring that the day was hot and the breeze non-existent. It felt good to sweat. It felt good to be so hot it was almost a form of torture. It felt good to fill her lungs with air and expel it so hard and fast everything burned.

At least now she knew she was alive. She ran for almost an hour before turning back towards her flat, and when she reached her street, she was so focused on the harsh ache in her lungs that she didn't notice the sleek black car parked in the narrow road, right outside her front door. As she got near it, though, the driver's door opened, and the sound caught her attention. She glanced across and stumbled, gasped, because there was Zeus Papandreo, looking intimidating and perfectly unbreakable, looking just as he had in her dreams, looking right back at her, and she stopped walking, with no idea what she could say, nor why he was here, but just knowing that she wasn't ready.

She couldn't face him.

'I'm— I need—' She pressed her fingers to her lips and took a step backwards, her face pale.

'Can we talk?'

She shook her head instinctively. On the one hand, she was desperate to talk to him some more, to do anything to spend time with him, but on the other, their last encounter had left her so badly bruised, she couldn't go through it again.

'I can't,' she whispered, dropping her head and staring at her feet. 'I want to, and I probably owe it to you, but I can't go through any more of that.' Her voice was barely above a mumble. 'I can't fight with you again.'

'I don't want to fight with you.'

A tear slid down her cheek. She flicked a glance at him. 'I don't believe you.'

His eyes slammed shut on a wave of emotions she couldn't interpret. 'I don't blame you.' He sighed. 'Listen, Jane, I was very angry that morning. I should have taken some time to get more facts, but I didn't. I took it out on you. I'm sorry.'

She shook her head quickly. 'More facts wouldn't have changed your mind. I did everything you accused me of.'

'You didn't lie to me,' he said, stepping closer towards her. 'Not about us. Everything we shared was real, and true, just like you said.'

She shook her head again. It was all too much. She didn't want to hear this, only to have him walk away and marry someone else. Did he have any notion how that idea had tortured her? The thought that he'd been engaged to someone else the whole time they'd been together? Having sex, as he'd so crudely put it. She took another step backwards, as if to repel that idea, and his features sharpened into a look of regret.

'Oh, Jane,' he sighed softly. 'If I could take back that morning—' he held his hands up, palms towards her, in a gesture of conciliation '—believe me, I would.'

She bit into her lower lip, heart popping like fizzing candy. She wanted to believe him, but how could she?

'The idea of having been lied to by *you*, the idea that I had been so damned foolish and mistaken what we were for something else entirely, it just made me feel so stupid. So angry. So hurt. And I took all of that out on you, instead of letting you explain. Instead of *hearing* what you were saying.'

'You did—'

'No, I mean really hearing you. Hearing you when you spoke about Charlotte's life, and how my father's choice to shield her from the world was a daily abandonment she has had to live with. How you saw that and moved in to mop up the pieces again and again, because even though she is strong and courageous, you see the same vulnerabilities in her that you feel in yourself. I wish I'd listened to you when you'd explained that she's your best friend, that you felt obligated to help her, even when you questioned the wisdom of her plan. And mostly, I wish I'd believed you when you said you wanted to change her mind, that you were planning to tell her that this was all wrong.'

Jane's eyes widened with shock and surprise. 'How did you—'

'Charlotte,' he said, dragging a hand through his hair. 'You got your wish. We ended up meeting, spending some time together these last couple of days. She made me see what a monumental ass I'd been. Which is why

I'm here.' His brow furrowed. 'Actually, I don't know if that's true. I suspect that even without Charlotte, I would have come to my senses eventually. She just dragged me there ahead of schedule.'

Jane blinked at him, her gut throbbing.

'I was never engaged to anyone else, Jane. I said that because I was lashing out. It is one of the biggest mistakes of my life. To know that I hurt you, that I inflicted that wound on you, because of my own pain, is something I will always be unbearably ashamed of.'

She groaned, dropping her head forward, because he *had* hurt her. Those words had tortured and tormented her every minute since. The prospect of him marrying— even when she'd contemplated that before.

'I didn't come here expecting that we could just get past this. I know it will take time. But I wanted to come to apologise first, and then to ask if you would even consider giving me another chance?'

Her head lifted of its own accord, her eyes locking to his.

And she felt all the uncertainty there—an uncharacteristic emotion for a man like Zeus—the sense that he was putting himself so far out on a limb for her. But Jane's heart was so battered, and her doubts so huge. Not about whether or not she loved him, but about what they could do next. For as much as he was begging for forgiveness, didn't she owe him the same?

'I wish I'd never agreed to do it,' she said softly, twisting her hands in front of her. 'But Charlotte was so sure—'

'And she's hard to say no to. I've seen it, believe me.'

A half smile lifted one side of Jane's mouth before dropping abruptly.

'If you hadn't agreed to it, we never would have met.' He closed the distance between them and this time, Jane held her ground, knowing he was going to touch her, and welcoming that. Needing it.

Slowly, so slowly she had time to avoid him if she wished it, he reached down and added his hand to hers, where they were still knotting at her front. 'From the moment we met, it was never about your promise to Charlotte, was it?'

Her eyes were round as they flew to his face, and she shook her head quickly. 'It was always about you.'

'And you,' he murmured, eyes dropping to her lips. 'And the kind of love that's rare and special and deserves to be fought for.'

Her breath rushed out of her lungs. 'Love?'

'Love. Obsession. Desire. Need.'

She laughed then, a laugh that was filled with the levity of a heart that was starting to glow with warmth once more. 'All that, huh?'

'And so much more. The kind of love that lasts a lifetime,' he promised, squeezing her hand then growing serious. 'Jane, before I found out about your connection to Charlotte, I felt as though I was walking on air, because I'd finally realised how I felt about you. I knew I'd met the love of my life, and that the kind of future I'd never allowed myself to hope for was suddenly all I could focus on. I had every intention of proposing to you that very morning, my *agapeméni*, in the shadows of the island that will soon be ours.'

Stars filled her vision, and she moved then, wrapping her arms around his waist and pulling him closer to her body. 'Is that your way of asking me to marry you, Zeus?'

'It's my way of *begging* you to relieve this enormous, crippling pain I've felt since you walked out of my life. How ever you can be in my world, whatever role you're willing to play, I want you there. I love you, and I am, and always will be, completely and utterly yours.'

A tear slid down her cheek, but for the first time since the yacht, this was a tear of joy, of giddy, blinding happiness and contentment. 'Well, then,' she murmured. 'I don't know how I could refuse,' she said, kissing him until her breath was burning in her lungs, a kiss that grew steadily more and more intense and passionate, so it was Zeus who pulled away, breathlessly, to suggest they move inside her flat rather than continue giving Hampstead a show.

And those were the last coherent words either of them spoke for several hours.

Afterwards, though, Jane realised there was one question she hadn't brought up. 'What will happen with the company?' Something heavy pressed against her chest, a weight that threatened to jeopardise the sheer joy she felt. 'I know it's yours, but at the same time, if our wedding meant Lottie couldn't be a part of it…'

'My father is having documents drawn as we speak. We cannot change the contracts of ownership, but we can redesign the organisational structure. I haven't discussed it with Charlotte yet, but my hope is that she'll agree to come on board with the Foundation, in the first instance. It seems like a natural fit.'

'Foundation?'

'I'm surprised I didn't mention it,' he said, his shoulder nudging hers. 'We run a large charity as part of our business, though I'm not surprised you're unaware. Silent philanthropy has always been important to my father, as it is to me. The charity is active in the US and much of Europe. As luck would have it, we're on the lookout for a director of operations. I think Charlotte would be perfect for the job.'

Jane's heart soared. 'Oh, she would be.'

'As would you,' he said, eyes roaming her face. 'There are other roles…'

She reached for his hand and squeezed it. 'I'll find another job,' she said. 'When I'm ready. But for now, if I'm completely honest, I'd like to focus on this.' She gestured from herself to him. 'For the first time in my life, I feel happy, and I feel loved, and I feel as though when I'm with you, I'm right exactly where I'm meant to be. I'd sort of like to just soak that up for a while. Does that sound weird?'

'*Agapaméni*, it sounds perfect.' And he reached down then, to the side of her bed, pulling his pants up and rifling through the pockets to remove a black velvet box. 'I didn't come here holding any hopes,' he promised. 'Well, maybe a very small hope, based on what a kind and forgiving, and generous-hearted angel you are. But if there was any chance that you might agree to marry me, I wanted to have this to give to you.'

He popped open the black velvet box to reveal an

enormous diamond ring encircled by sapphires. 'It was my grandmother's,' he said, voice a little thick.

Her eyes were filled with moisture as she extended a shaking hand towards him, so that he could slip the ring in place. It fit like a glove.

'I have my mother's ring, too, but my father has asked that he be allowed to give that to you—to welcome you to the family.'

'The family,' she breathed out, and then fell back against Zeus's chest, a smile stretched from ear to ear. Yes, she was just perfectly, exactly where she wanted to be.

* * * * *

If Billion-Dollar Dating Deception
*left you wanting more,
then don't miss the next instalment in the
A Greek Inheritance Game duet*
Tycoon's Terms of Engagement
coming next month!

*And why not explore these other stories
from Clare Connelly?*

His Runaway Royal
Pregnant Before the Proposal
Unwanted Royal Wife
Billion-Dollar Secret Between Them
Twins for His Majesty

Available now!

HARLEQUIN
Reader Service

Enjoyed your book?

Try the perfect subscription for Romance readers and get more great books like this delivered right to your door.

See why over 10+ million readers have tried Harlequin Reader Service.

Start with a Free Welcome Collection with free books and a gift—valued over $20.

Choose any series in print or ebook.
See website for details and order today:

TryReaderService.com/subscriptions